SEASON OF DEATH

In the grip of a killing drought, the cattle lands became a near-waterless nightmare. Cattlemen and farmers alike pulled out to seek new lives elsewhere. Jim Crown was no less anxious to quit that place of death, but brutal events intervened and he was drawn into a blazing conflict with the deadly Billy Grieve. This was to be a fight to the death, and the vicious climax was fought out in a raging dust storm.

LEE F. GREGSON

SEASON OF DEATH

Complete and Unabridged

LINFORD
Leicester

First published in Great Britain in 1992 by
Robert Hale Limited
London

First Linford Edition
published August 1995
by arrangement with
Robert Hale Limited
London

British Library CIP Data

Gregson, Lee F.
    Season of death.—Large print ed.—
Linford western library
I. Title II. Series
823.914 [F]

ISBN 0–7089–7753–7

Published by
F. A. Thorpe (Publishing) Ltd.
Anstey, Leicestershire

Set by Words & Graphics Ltd.
Anstey, Leicestershire
Printed and bound in Great Britain by
T. J. Press (Padstow) Ltd., Padstow, Cornwall

This book is printed on acid-free paper

' . . . there fell
on trees and crops a hideous plague,
a season of death.'

VIRGIL: *The Aeneid*, Book III

1

THAT year, during the very worst of it, up on Reever's they shot big-ribbed cattle, and all along the dried-up bed of the Cimrie River, those beasts that had not died among tinder-dry brush and under choking, spiralling dust, lay bloating on the smooth, bared boulders of the Cimrie, after their final, staggering, despairing search for water.

It was the second year of searing drought, and following on from two years of poor prices for beef, it had become the killing blow for a good many of the cattle outfits in that part of the country, ranches no longer able to raise anything fit to drive, in numbers, to anywhere. Even the bigger spreads were hurting, the more so those unable to negotiate further bank credits; but it had been crippling for most of the smaller spreads and for almost all of the homesteaders who had been scattered along the fringe of what once had been the life-giving Cimrie. It was as though the world itself was in the process of dying, and the hot wind that seemed to blow ceaselessly was in fact the foul breath of Hell itself.

When one by one the outfits began to fold, those men who were the lucky ones were paid their time; others, and there were numbers of them from ranches worse hit, simply had to pull their picket pins and leave, with wages owing, and with bitter resentments gnawing at them; simple men, some of them, disappointed yet philosophical, others dangerous, turned out now to survive as best they might all through the ravaged, dying land.

The towns, what towns there were, and such as they were, suffered too, became sad, heat-curled huddles, swept by the burning wind, raked by dust, for days on end moving only with desolate, rolling tumbleweeds, blown from wilderness on their way to wilderness.

Old trusts were dying along with the land, the cattle and the once-green vegetation. Men developed the habit of looking over their shoulders and of watching carefully the eyes of others they encountered. Yet, as in all times of human trial and vicissitude, some still clung to hope of better days, others to faith beyond hope, albeit a faith now often threadbare. In the ironically named town of Hope, the small clapboard church still rang sometimes to the singing of worshippers, though by now fewer in number.

'The morning shall awaken,
The shadows shall decay,
And each true-hearted servant
Shall shine as doth the day.'

Of the three once bustling saloons in the town, only one, The Cattleman's, remained open for such sporadic business as was offering; more often nowadays it came from riders or wagoners passing through Hope on their way to anywhere at all that was not dried, brown and dusty and raked by the filthy wind. The Cattleman's, though it no longer shipped in supplies of liquor, was managing to survive not only by virtue of its own stocks, but by residual ones abandoned by the owners of the other two establishments, who had departed long ago on creaking stages, eastward. There was a livery in the town still, a feed and grain, now all but bare, a general store with dwindling stocks and a hopeless For Sale notice pasted on its large, single window fronting Main. Bessemer's Hotel still had its doors open, but inside was not much more than an echoing shell; and there were a few other assorted businesses, among them a barbershop, for all the barber had in the world was invested in the enterprise, and there were, of course, no interested buyers. The whores though, always few in number in the town of

Hope, had long ago gone to seek out richer pickings elsewhere. As far as Hope was concerned, and the town of Albertine sixty miles north-west of it, the terrible drought across the cattle lands had become more like a plague that in the end must infect everything and everyone, and, it seemed, must eventually kill everything and everyone as well.

Maybe the worst thing that had happened, though it had not yet become universally apparent, was that because the towns, like many of the ranches, had no money, they could no longer afford to pay to keep the peace. Albertine's town marshal had been clubbed down in a brawl outside one of the saloons, months ago, and had died without regaining consciousness, and nobody else had fancied taking on the job, one with much risk and little prospect of recompense; and the man who had represented the law in Hope had simply closed the door of the office and jail one morning and had climbed aboard the noon eastbound stage with the last of the whores. All of which meant that the nearest law of any sort was near to a hundred and fifty miles away and anyway had enough to concern itself with nearer home. There had been a telegraph office in Hope, but it, like so many other things, no longer operated.

So all of that territory rimmed on the one side by the jagged shapes of the Osterman Range, all down the long valleys and across the once-rich rangelands of the Halle Flats, sweeping down to the great curve of what had been the Cimrie River under the Flinter Hills, was like a wasteland, unworked and unwanted and open to predators of every conceivable kind.

2

IN brush-strewn, rocky country about halfway between Hope and Albertine, a man and his wife and child, a girl of maybe twelve, had made a camp in a clearing among a scattering of lumpy boulders, had made a small meal, the child being given the best portion, and now they were resting, all three, in the shade of the wagon. They still had about half a canteen of the warm, gritty water that they had obtained from the last of the deep wells in Hope, and that, grudgingly, and mainly because of the presence of the big-eyed child. But there was no more to be had for the pair of wagon-horses, and the man, Sellers, thought that unless the animals could be found some by at least this time tomorrow, he might just as well abandon any idea of pressing on beyond Albertine.

"We'll wait here 'til sundown, then if the moon's as good as it was last night we'll take advantage of the cool air and move on to Augustine."

A tall, rawboned man in his mid-thirties, Sellers, and his eyes already showed the dullness that was made of a kind of defeat; indeed it was the look of a man who has played all of his best cards, and knows it, and still, against all expectations, has lost the game. His wife, sitting on the ground by the wagon, flapping a small linen cloth in front of her shining face, out of habit rather than with any real hope of cooling herself, was a once-pretty but now work-faded woman, her dark, braided hair pinned up, a small, flat little bonnet atop of it, a flap down over the back of her neck, the headgear tied under her chin.

"And what then, when we do get to Albertine?"

Sellers, leathery-skinned, eyes slitted by dust and distance, pinkish vest and old moleskin trousers, pulled the wide brim of his hat further down and hunched, round-shouldered, near her.

"We'll need to see how it is in Albertine. Any drink fer the horses. What the prospects are. Can't make any other plans out here."

The young girl, pinched little face under her blue bonnet, bright, questing eyes shifting from one parent to the other, said nothing. The only home she had known, the small-holding down on the Cimrie River, now lay far behind them, and all they had in the world that had not been too heavy to move, was stacked in the wagon above her. Down here, where they were, they had at least some protection from the direct, hammering heat of the sun, and a modicum of shelter from the searching wind that for days on end had whipped grainy dust through wagon and contents, bedding and clothing, until the whole world seemed nothing more than unrelenting heat and grit.

"Other plans," the woman said, picking up on him, her voice low and toneless, neither approving nor disapproving, though he was himself unsettled, and sensed criticism.

"What else can we do, Maida? You tell me what else."

She coughed drily, flapping her cloth at darting flies, tugged at the bonnet of the child, who drew her head away sharply.

"I didn't say we should do aught else."

"Well then." They fell into a brooding silence, pestered by flies. Somewhere on the wagon loose canvas flapped in the wind, a disconsolate sound, and that was all for some while until the thin, reedy voice of the child broke in.

"I'm still real hungry."

The man looked up from studying his boots, made as though to rise, but a minute gesture from the woman checked him.

"Wait a while longer, Lily. Wait 'til near sundown. There's bacon left an' plenty o' the bread, an' some of the bottled things. We'll get ourselves a little something before we set out for Albertine."

"From Hope to Albertine, and hope," thought Sellers sourly.

The child made as though to speak again but the sight of a finger at her mother's lips was sufficient to make her change her mind. Lily's small face went down and she hunched her bladed shoulders over, as though by doing so she might somehow find further protection from the dust.

★ ★ ★

Crown, coming slowly down a long, brushy slope some good distance off, walking the horse, husbanding its strength, saw a wagon in a clearing between boulders, though at first he could distinguish no-one near it; then he believed he could make out a group of figures sitting almost underneath it. He drew rein, the dry wind tugging at him, his slitted eyes studying the far-off rig, its pair of horses standing immobile with a suggestion of drooping heads. Crown began to think about what might be his best line of ride from where he now was, knowing that some thirty miles away to his right lay the town of Hope, and that a similar distance in the opposite direction was Albertine. He figured that there would be little to choose between them, though beyond Hope lay all that remained of the Cimrie. Ordinarily that in itself would be no recommendation, but beyond that again were the Flinter Hills and it had been in his mind to press on down there and eventually to cross them while the bay horse was still capable of doing it; once over the barrier of those hills, even though he had but small expectations of immediately discovering better conditions, seventy, eighty miles further on might bring him to a more agreeable climate. Unless the entire country was running out of water, and there was really nothing to indicate to him that such might not be the case. One thing he was quite certain of; he did not want anything to do with the wagon. A couple of days back he had approached one and some real touchy bastard had opened up on him with a rifle, and although every shot fell short, Crown had veered away at once and put some distance and eventually some monolithic rocks between himself and the shooter, angry, yet in some measure understanding of such a poor reception. Deep suspicion was fast becoming part of the fabric of this dying world and meant that a man had to discipline himself even more strictly than usual, make any approaches to strangers encountered on the trail with great circumspection.

Having come to a halt to study the distant wagon he thought that this spot would be as good as any to allow the horse a drink of his precious water, so he swung down, unshipped the canteen and poured some of its warmish contents into his hat. The horse took the water readily and looked for more but Crown rubbed its nose and slapped the wet hat back on his head, thongs hanging either side of his leathery face.

"Enough for now, boy, even though it wasn't near enough."

Up in the saddle again, ducking his head against a blow of dust, he was about to nudge the horse on, to strike out in a direction which would take him well wide of the wagon and its people, when he thought he glimpsed movement of some kind 'way off to his right, and lower down, on the flats where the lone wagon was. Crown steadied the horse, muttering to it, squinting into distance, gloved hand raised to protect his already raw eyes. Yes, there it was again, dust that was not merely wind-raised dust. Riders. Crown allowed the horse to slow a little, turning its head away from the worst of the wind, and he himself sat with his body twisted to the side, not taking his attention from the group — for definitely there was more

14

than one horseman coming — and he could see as they drew nearer that their line of ride must take them close to the wagon. Still no-one was stirring near that vehicle, the horses still standing heads down, and Crown could only surmise that whoever they were down there, they were unaware of the approaching horsemen.

The riders could be discerned more clearly now; there were three of them and Crown watched with no more than idle interest as, evidently noticing the standing wagon, they altered their direction slightly to head towards it, weaving in and out of brush and boulders, followed and overhung by their own considerable dust that was being lifted by a following wind. Even though, perhaps fewer than a hundred yards short of the wagon they brought their horses down to a walk, it must have been the thickening dust that caused somebody to look, and that brought about sudden activity at the wagon. Both hands now cupped over his eyebrows, concentrating, Crown thought at first there were two people down there, then realized that there were three, one much smaller than the others. Two adults and one child. One of the taller figures seemed to be climbing up on the wagon but as the riders drew closer in, got down again and then all three began backing away. Crown caught the glint of something on one of the horsemen and assumed it to be a drawn gun. A worm of unease stirred in his stomach as he watched the mounted group come right in on the wagon and draw to a halt.

★ ★ ★

The woman could smell them even from where she was standing, men and horses; hard, ugly men, one showing brown-stained teeth when he saw her looking. Old, threadbare clothing they had on, that had not seen any washing in a long while, thorn-raked and patched leather chaps over their trousers, sweat-stained dusty shirts of dull grey material, an assortment of old, greasy, shapeless hats with wide brims, and boots that were in need of repair. All were slung with pistols, the one who had had the drawn gun having slid it back in the holster when he got a closer look at the wagoners. The three horses, sweat-rimed and dusty, stood in docile fashion, probably thankful for a brief pause in travelling.

All three newcomers studied the man first, classed him — rightly as it turned out — as a homesteader from somewhere, now on the move, a big fellow who looked as though he was a tough one, even though he and those with him had taken a pace or two away as their visitors had approached. And before that, the man had immediately got down off the side of the wagon when called upon to do so. They shifted their attention from the man to the two females with him, the woman pretty fair looking, they thought, and though small, well made, for the wind was pressing her clothing hard against her body. The third one was a young girl of perhaps twelve, thirteen, coming into early womanhood, small-boned, perkily pretty, buffeted by the wind, looking uncertainly from the mounted men to her pa.

One of the horsemen, named Ollerman, showed some more of his dirty teeth, frankly appraising the woman and the girl, then shifting his gaze back to the man.

"Pullin' out, friend?" His voice had a high-pitched note to it; a squawky voice.

"That's it," said the homesteader, Sellers. "Nothin' left fer us out here."

"Where be ye from?" asked Ollerman.

"Place called Ritter's, down on the Cimrie."

"Uh-huh. Uh-huh. Dirt farmer, huh?"

Sellers nodded. He had not made up his mind about them yet but thought he did not much care for the looks of them, in particular the man who had asked the questions.

18

"Same all over," Ollerman said. "Same all over." His foxy eyes moved to the woman again. "An' this would be the loyal wife. No doubt of it. A flower in the near desert." His attention shifted again. "An' the little bud." One of the others sniggered. Sellers knew with a draining certainty that they indeed meant trouble and he wished to God he had managed to get the Henry out of the wagon. Even as that thought came into his mind, as though in some strange way it had conveyed itself to these men sitting on their hard-worked horses, one of them, thick-set and bushy-bearded, nudged his horse and moved across to the wagon, peering inside the front of it under the hooped canvas just behind the seat. To Sellers' dismay he then swung one leg over the horse's head and casually stepped across onto the wagon and leaned in. When he turned and just as easily remounted the horse, he was holding the Henry by its barrel.

"Now look what ol' sodbuster was

19

after when we come along."

Sellers spread his hands. "Warn't sure who it was comin'."

"Uh-huh. Uh-huh," said Ollerman. "That's true. Ye never do know fer sure who it is comin'." He laughed then and his companions joined in, the bearded man holding the rifle aloft and the third man, with the pale, freckled face of a redhead, slapped one of his knees enthusiastically.

The woman felt that she wanted to run but her feet felt as though they had been pegged to the ground. Anyway, she thought, if she did move her knee joints would give way and she would fall.

Ollerman, without turning his head, spoke to the freckled man.

"Purdie, hitch the hosses." At that, Ollerman and the bearded man dismounted and Purdie moved to attend to the horses, first hitching his own to the tailgate of the wagon.

Once on the ground, Ollerman and the bearded man walked nearer to the homesteader and his wife and daughter. The bearded man then looked absently at the old Henry as though suddenly wondering why he was holding it, then tossed it on the ground near the wagon.

"What is it yuh want of us?" Sellers heard himself asking. "We ain't got much water."

"Uh-huh," said Ollerman.

"We're hopin' to git us some more in Albertine."

"Uh-huh," said Ollerman again. Then: "Wa-al, sodbuster, it ain't water we need. Sure, we could allers use some more, no doubt of it; but we been somewhat lucky with water, one way an' another. No. It's more the fact that we been on the trail a fair good while now, an' to put it plain, it's been a long time between women, an' I don't reckon we could last out 'til Albertine."

Instinctively, hopelessly, Sellers went across in front of his wife and child and both Ollerman and the bearded

21

man wasted no more time and at once fell upon him. From where he was near the wagon-gate, securing the other two horses, Purdie called:

"Save me one with the li'l gal, Oller! I shore do fancy somethin' that smells fresher'n a N'Mexico whore!"

The woman had grabbed the girl by the hand and now turned to run, though where she thought she might go was not clear. Sellers was proving to be no pushover, however, and they were still struggling violently with him, and Ollerman had in fact just dropped a hand to the butt of his pistol, trying to help keep hold of Sellers with the other one, when Purdie shouted:

"Rider comin'!"

When Ollerman and everybody else looked, Crown, coming steadily through the dust, was about a hundred feet away, a big man on a deep-chested bay, reins around his left wrist, that same arm raised and crooked, a rifle resting across it; and as soon as they all became aware of Crown he stopped the walking horse. To Ollerman and his companion, Crown called:

"Step back! Step away from him!" Ollerman did take a couple of paces away from Sellers but clearly it was a move designed to give himself room to clear the pistol away for a shot at Crown. "Don't be a fool!" Crown shouted. Ollerman stood still, Purdie, with the horses, had not made any moves, but the bearded man now looked around for the discarded Henry, and when he saw it, took a few lumbering steps and stooped for it.

The lashing report of Crown's rifle was flattened somewhat by the wind but nonetheless it caused the horses in Purdie's charge to move around and the wagon horses raise their heads and the young girl put her hands to her ears and turned her face in towards her mother as the black bearded man coming upright with the Henry in his hands was slammed back against one of the wagon's wheels as though he had been given a two-handed hit with a spade. He was still gripping the rifle but it was a stiff, tightening grip, as though he now simply wanted something solid to hang onto. Then he slid down with his back propped against the wagon wheel, his bushy face sinking down onto a chest that was spreading with blood.

"That was a damn' fool thing for him to try," Crown said. His horse was walking forward again. The right-side brim of his hat was being pushed flat by the wind but the hat was now firmly thonged under his jaw. In slow steps, as Crown advanced, Ollerman was backing away and Purdie was well occupied with his fractious horses. "Stand still," Crown said to Ollerman. Ollerman stood. He looked as though he badly wanted to slit Crown's throat but he was not such a fool as to try anything under the killing threat of the rifle. "Turn about," said Crown. Ollerman turned. Leather creaked as Crown dismounted and crossed to him and lifted the heavy pistol from

Ollerman's holster and held it out to one side to have Sellers step forward and take it. Sellers' lower lip was split and there was a run of bright blood from one of his nostrils. To Purdie, who now looked as though he might be on the brink of committing a foolish act of his own, Crown said: "Don't you ever learn anything?" Purdie let the tension drain out of his body and came forward slowly and allowed himself to be disarmed. "Now," said Crown to Purdie, "go fetch Blackbeard's horse and walk it along the side of the wagon, an' then you an' him," indicating Ollerman, "you an' him hoist him up over the saddle an' tie him there."

"We ought to bury him," Ollerman said.

"That would be wise," said Crown, "in fact I'd strongly advise it, but you'll take him well out of our sight to do it. Now set about putting him on that horse."

It took them some ten minutes to get it done and get themselves up and

C.1

ready to move out.

"What about the pistols?" Ollerman asked. "Yuh cain't turn us loose without nothin', not out here."

"I could," Crown said. "I could keep your cayuses an' your boots as well, an' make you tow him away afoot, but I won't. The gun that was Blackbeard's stays here along with his shellbelt an' the Bowie out of his boot." They watched as he unloaded first Ollerman's pistol, then Purdie's. "These, you can have back, unloaded. I'm going to ride along with you for maybe a quarter of a mile, an' after that, you'll go on an' I'll watch you out of my sight, an' if I think you or him seems to be reloading, I'll put up the sights of this rifle here an' blow a hole in you that we could drive this whole rig through. You understand me?" Ollerman said he did, but his expression, the way his eyes were, said he was marking Crown's every feature, burning them into his mind. "Then go," said Crown.

26

They followed the direction he insisted upon, a route at right angles to that which would be followed by Sellers and his wagon, and in fact, set them at the rising ground down which Crown had made his approach. Ollerman and Purdie led out, towing the horse with the jouncing body of the black bearded man on it, then came Crown, the butt of the rifle braced on his right knee as he rode. At the top of the rise when, to Sellers and his woman at the wagon, they were only specks, Crown came to a halt and remained up there for the best part of half an hour, then turned the bay around, leaned back to scabbard the rifle, and took his time going on back down to the wagon.

The homesteader shook his hand.

"Will Sellers."

"Jim Crown."

Sellers studied him a moment as though some faint memory had stirred, but he could not reach it and mentally shrugged the wraith of it away. He introduced his wife, Maida, and his daughter, Lily.

"The men come on us out o' nowhere," the woman said.

"We wasn't keepin' a good look out," said Sellers. "There's allers been dangerous men around, out here; now there are more of 'em than ever there was, an' others, good men once, gone to the bad. It's a hard lesson we've been given. We mustn't ever fergit it."

"It was a bad thing to have to do," Crown said, "killing the man. But when he got hold of the rifle he left me no choice. We'd all have been dead by now."

"Will they come back?" This time it was the girl's voice, thin and high, still a frightened voice.

"I doubt it," Crown said. "They can't be sure we won't all stay together an' they can't risk coming onto two rifles." He turned again to Sellers. "Have you come from Hope?"

"Yeah. Headin' for Albertine. There was some water to be had in Hope,

28

but not much. Water's a matter o' pure luck. The Cimrie's near to dry an' all the cricks sure are, leadin' off it; but in under the Flinters, one or two got wells that I know of with some small amounts o' water still comin'. Depends on the kind o' well. Some that are real deep are the ones. Some o' them streams underground flow one hell of a ways; but even outfits that do still have water ain't got a lot of it, an' there'd be some that wouldn't admit to havin' any, anyway."

"Can't blame 'em for that," Crown said. "There'd never be enough for everybody that wanted it."

"Mebbe not," Sellers said. "An' I got no call to complain. Like I said, in Hope they let me have some, mostly on account o' the girl."

Lily had been staring solemnly at the big rider all the while. The eyes of the woman were fixed on him too, taking in every detail of his range clothing and his good looking but slightly scarred face under the shallow black hat that he wore. He had come unhesitatingly to their aid when they had most needed it, yet there was something about him, the way he looked, the way he carried himself, the way he spoke, that disturbed her, even chilled her; and he had killed a man right down here at their wagon, and there was dark blood on the ground from that. She was thankful for Crown yet wanted to see the back of him at the same time. With a stab almost of guilt she saw that his gunmetal stare had become fixed on her and he had said something that she had not caught. In response to her blank, then confused look, he repeated it.

"If you're planning on going to Albertine tonight, by the moon, you'll need to watch your back trail. After sundown the wind should drop away, so dust won't be a problem."

She nodded. "Me an' Lily will sit back in the wagon an' keep a watch out."

"And fires;" he said to Sellers, "if

you should see fires, veer away from them. If you have to, get down an' lead your team if you're not certain of the footing or want to keep noise down."

Sellers nodded. "You ain't goin' to Albertine, obviously."

Crown shook his head. "I've a notion to cross the Flinter Hills, maybe head on up to Saffron, around there."

"Then I wish yuh well," said Sellers.

"Go with care," said Crown.

They gripped hands, and Crown, with a nod and a touch of his hat to the woman and to Lily, mounted up and turned away without another word, and from the wagon they watched horse and rider until they became swallowed up by the coursing dust and the shimmering waves of heat.

3

THE whole outfit was empty, baking under the unforgiving sun, dry and dust-covered. He wondered where the inhabitants might have gone, abandoning a place like this. Up through Albertine, very likely, and then on again, north of that place, just as Sellers and his people intended to do. It had been a smallish spread, maybe not up to much at the best of times. There was a not over-large ranch-house, a bunkhouse, a barn, one or two other nondescript lean-to affairs and two corrals.

Crown hitched his horse to a pole of the corral nearest to the main building and walked across to the back porch, calling, yet knowing instinctively that he was calling to a dead house. There was a lost look of abandonment all around the hard-packed yard and the buildings baking in the heat, flies buzzing, the faint smell of animals still permeating everything; yet no cattle to be seen, no horses, and all around as far as the eye could see, the brush and rock-strewn country was shimmering with sun and misted distance right to the greyish huddle of his first objective, the Flinter Hills.

Heavy-hearted, Crown stood surveying it all, now wondering if indeed his plan to find his way over the Flinters and beyond, was the best course for him to take. He glanced again at the house, knowing that soon he must somehow find more water, if not for himself then for the animal he rode. About half a canteen remained. He would drink sparingly, let the horse have the remainder, gamble that there would be enough to get him across the hills and gamble again that he would find more water on the other side of them. He reckoned that he had come too far to alter his plan now; and unlike others, he had no great faith in Albertine and what might lie beyond that town.

Purely out of curiosity he entered the house. On bare, gritty floors he walked slowly through the empty rooms. The people who had once lived here must have had wagons at their disposal, for the interior had been stripped of all furniture, and all closets and cupboards had been emptied, some of their doors left standing open. A few minor items had been forgotten, a few candle-stubs left and a broken oil lamp, a few pieces of cutlery and a tin mug. He went out of the house and casually toured the other buildings. Apart from straw bales in the barn and a filthy, discarded pair of longjohns in the bunkhouse, a place which still retained its human stench, there was nothing. Certainly no water, though there was a well covered over by a lean-to near the barn; but when he dropped a pebble into it he heard it go rattling all the way down to strike upon other stones.

It was late in the afternoon and he did consider bunking down in this place for he was in need of rest, but in the end decided to move on, perhaps continue travelling through the greater part of the night, for the nearer he could get to the Flinter Hills while the horse was still moving well, the better.

He swung up into the sun-hot saddle and went on his way, taking his time, moving at a walk through clumps of dry, spiky brush, and he had just passed from further sight of the abandoned ranch buildings when he heard the sound of riders. They were still some little distance away, well behind him, but he pulled the horse to a halt and turned it, moving slowly to a place where he could look back cautiously.

Though he was now some distance away he could see that there were four riders arriving in the yard of the ranch as he himself had done, calling out — for he could hear the faint cries — then dismounting, one man remaining with the horses, the others climbing the steps onto the porch and going inside. Crown had no wish to be seen by them, so once more turned the horse about and moved it away at a walk. As he progressed steadily through tinder-dry brush he took good care to raise as little dust as possible, glancing back from time to time and all the while listening for the approach of riders; but none came. As the distance between himself and the forlorn ranch and its visitors became greater, gradually he began to relax his caution about his back-trail and gave more attention to the arid country which he had yet to cross.

Perhaps an hour after he had seen the riders, however, and perhaps through some instinct engendered by years of surviving in this wild land, he again drew to a halt and looked back the way he had come, though the abandoned ranch was now far behind him and out of sight.

Smoke was standing far up into the pure blue sky, smoke that was being pushed urgently by some fierce blaze, and now when he looked more carefully, he could see that it seemed to have several sources, though close enough together to join and form into a single rich, rolling plume. Crown realized at once, by the direction, what those sources would be. Whoever the riders had been, they had not seen fit simply to make an inspection of the place, then ride on their way; they had fired the ranch-house and all its out-buildings. Sick at heart, Crown sat on his saddle watching for several minutes before continuing on his own journey. Derelict or not, the place once had been the centre of somebody's ambitions and hopes, and in the fullness of time might have been so again, for someone else. The destruction of it was needless and without point, yet he knew, was symbolic of the new, embittered way of life that had settled like the killing drought itself, upon this beleaguered and dispirited land.

Towards evening, though the red-veiled sun had sunk away, waves of heat were still pulsing from the parched earth. Crown emerged from between skeletal trees into a stony clearing and at once hauled up. Fifty yards ahead, near the farther end of this open space, beyond which lay more ragged brush, then a wide valley between low spurs of the Flinters, three unsaddled horses were picketed. Their riders, saddles and bedrolls and other belongings strewn around, were in the process of making camp, one man crouched over some scraps of brush which had been arranged inside a ring of stones, and in the act of setting a light to it. The fire blazed up readily and so swiftly that the man who had lit it had to duck his head away. So intent were all three on the making of the camp that they did not immediately notice the motionless horseman at the far end of the clearing. When one of them did, and said something sharply, they spread out at once, six feet or so

38

separating each, facing him. All were armed but none made any move to draw a weapon.

Crown raised his left palm, held it there a moment, lowered it slowly and began to walk the horse towards them. He had had no desire even to talk with anyone but calculated that he would have been unable to withdraw from sight without having been seen and perhaps fired on. The campfire continued blazing, a thin finger of blue-grey smoke rising high, curved away by the wind. Thirty feet short of them, Crown stopped the horse.

"Passin' through," Crown said. "Didn't expect to come across anybody out here."

They were a tough-looking lot, one a lanky individual with a finely-wrinkled face and whitish eyebrows, the one next to him a tall, powerful man, chest straining at his shirt, with a round, flushed face and very small dark eyes; and the third more sparely built, with a nose that had been broken at some time, and with a drooping ginger moustache. All were wearing clothing that was very old, dirty and in poor repair; all had on hard-used leather chaps over moleskin trousers, and all were slung with gunbelts and carried heavy pistols in darkly greasy holsters. Crown judged them at first to be range men who, like many others, had been thrown out of work, yet there was another, uneasy aspect to them when he studied them, that might just as easily mark them as men who might not have worked cattle in some while, not for wages, anyway, gone to the bad long ago. If that impression was accurate, then they were dangerous.

"No more did we, mister," the man with the moustache said. Three pairs of hard eyes were fixed unblinkingly on the mounted man, absorbing every detail of horse and rider, matching his appearance, no doubt, to their own conceived notions of who or what he might be; uncertain, suspicious. "Since yuh're here, yuh'd best light down."

The range courtesy was in the words only, a grudging note in the tone, but Crown walked the horse another few steps and swung down. None of the three offered names, nor did Crown. After a pause the white-eyebrowed man spoke in a curiously sing-song voice:

"We got beans an' some bacon but not much water."

"I've got some water left," said Crown easily, "but not a lot." It turned out that he certainly had more water than they had between the three of them, so he made coffee as his contribution to the meal, while the lanky, wrinkled man set about preparing the food. There was a muttering surliness about them that did not appeal to Crown at all, but he decided he would simply have his supper at this camp, then move on, for he had no wish to pass the night in their company.

An hour later, when they were all sitting cross-legged around the fire, he flicked the dregs of his coffee into the flames and stood up, stowing utensils in his warbag. Earlier, he had not unsaddled the horse, merely loosened the cinches and now, probably surprisingly to the three still at the fire, set about tightening them again.

"Obliged to you for the meal and the company," said Crown. "Now I have to move on."

Indeed they had expected to see him unsaddle and picket the horse for the night for they now exchanged quick glances. The one with the moustache stood up stiffly, looking at Crown near his horse on the edge of the firelight.

"Not a good time for travellin', friend, in this kind of country."

Crown shrugged. "Better now than in the heat of the day, when a man doesn't know where the next water will be," he said. "And there's a good moon." He was aware that the other two were now standing but they had not moved from the fire.

"That water yuh still got," the moustached man said then, "we'd deem it kindly to git us a drop fer at least one o' the canteens."

So that was it. Crown finished tightening the cinches, straightened up.

"I've got some distance still to go," he said, "an' what there is, is for the horse."

The bulky, small-eyed one spoke for the first time, in the husky voice of a fat man.

"What yuh got left would wet four whistles jes' nice," he said, "but it wouldn't hardly be enough to damp his tongue."

Crown shrugged again.

"Nevertheless, it's his water."

"Look," said the one with the moustache, "we come near a hunnert an' fifty mile in this shit of an oven on three canteens that wasn't full to begin with. Now, a cupful all 'round ain't askin' a lot an' it would help us git to Albertine where we've got a mind to go."

Crown flicked a glance towards their

picketed animals standing shining in the moonlight, and they seemed to him to be reasonably fresh considering the distance these men said they had come, but he said:

"If I had a near full canteen you'd be welcome to half, but I don't have that much. What I do have is his." He slapped the horse's neck lightly. "That way he just might not die under me on the way to where I'm going."

The round-faced man spoke up again.

"That yore last word?"

"That's my last word." He thought that if any of them tried anything it would be the one with the moustache, but in the event it was the man with the white eyebrows whose hand dropped to the butt of his Colt; but he got no further, for when Crown's hand dipped it came up with his own long pistol in it and it had been smooth enough to make them all blink. "Pull that thing an' you're a fool," said Crown. At first he had not believed that they would go that far for the comparatively small amount of water that he was carrying but, he was compelled to reflect, in times such as these there could be no accounting for the actions of some men; like the senseless burning of the abandoned ranch. Eyebrows lifted his hand away from the butt of the gun with fastidious care.

"Kinda touchy ain't yuh, mister?"

"There are plenty of places," said Crown evenly, "where you'd be staring at a hole in your belly by now, an' you know that well enough." During the meal he had taken some note of their possessions lying scattered about, and had noticed no rifle anywhere. That was something. In fact that very thing might well turn out to be of paramount importance for, still watching them and holding the gun, as he swung up into the saddle, the round-faced man said:

"Yuh won't git far."

"We'll see," said Crown. He thought that once he was out of sight of their camp they would think better of it;

45

but he took great pains in walking the horse to the edge of the clearing while still turned half around in the saddle and the gun still drawn. Even without benefit of firelight the three figures would have been sharply defined under the milk-white moon. Hardly had he passed from their view, however, than there came the boom of a shot and the slug crashed among the dry brush not far from him. Crown, however, did not hurry himself unduly, knowing that if they did come after him they must first saddle their horses, so he picked his way with care, very soon passing into a wide valley that marked the extremities of the Flinter Hills, though those hills proper were in fact some miles ahead. He had not covered much more than three hundred yards, however, having no difficulty in finding a safe route, when he became aware that they really were coming after him.

Soon he discovered how deep and wide this valley was, and though there was still plenty of spiky brush to be avoided, it had to some extent thinned out so that he was able to kick the horse along with more confidence, trusting that the footing would remain good, yet conscious of the fact that in bright moonlight there was little chance of his getting far without being seen. And it did not take long to happen. They must have saddled up fast and got out after him at a dead run, risking being raked to shreds as they rode. He heard the shouting of the group far behind him carrying clearly through the night and a lone gun went off, but as yet the range was too great. Nonetheless he urged the big horse to stretch out and did not turn his head to look behind but concentrated solely on the way ahead.

It was when he rounded a clay shoulder that jutted from the side of the valley, that he realized that he was for the moment out of sight of his pursuers, and his eyes probed the shadows seeking out any possible place where he might manage to conceal himself in the hope that they would

47

ride on by and so give him the opportunity to double back. Crown had an uneasy feeling about this valley, suspecting that it might well lead him into some unclimbable dead end and leave him facing the very real danger of three guns; and he cursed the necessity to make the horse expend so much of its strength, knowing that it must soon be in dire need of water, and that the small quantity he had left would not be nearly enough. No obvious place to hide could he see, so he rode on, feeling exposed in the white brightness of the moon, thankful for deep shadows when from time to time they appeared. He decided to risk coming to a stop so that he could listen for the pursuit, and so, the horse heaving and blowing under him, its head tossing, side-stepping, Crown moving to steady and reassure it, he did listen. Certainly, there was the sound of their running horses, and they had gained on him. And there they were, perhaps three hundred yards away. There was no option. He clapped spurs in and was away once more, leaning down over the neck of the horse as he rode.

They must have seen movement for he heard faint cries and for the second time a gun went off. Crown let the big bay run. Two hundred yards further up the big valley, on some sort of faint trail, he swept again around a shoulder in the valley side and found himself passing through brush and clumps of trees, and fifty yards beyond that, saw a jumble of large boulders, some of the gaps between them open, others choked with dense brush, and knowing that he must get in under cover, took his chance and headed his hard-run horse through one of the dark apertures and into a small, shadowy space, beyond which stood bigger stones and more ragged brush. Crown drew the horse to a halt. He got down and went to the head of the bay, clasping it, talking in a low voice, aware of the fact that it was tired, pushed as far as he would now permit it to be pushed. To hell with them. This was as far as he was going; they could do what they liked. And it was not the matter of the water, he was quite sure. It was more likely to be an enraged bloody-mindedness, a desire to revenge themselves upon him because he had bested them, seen through them at the camp. For these three were not simple men of the range, they were hard-noses, rustlers perhaps in their time, always chancers, predators too, whenever an opportunity should arise, and men who were not content to accept an affront. Over the years, Crown had met many like them, all across the west, and knew that if they found him he was in for a hell of a fight.

4

WITHIN a very few minutes, still holding the horse and standing motionless, straining to hear the sounds of the horsemen, he became aware that they had ridden on past the place where he had chosen to wait. Though the small, almost enclosed space to some extent deadened noises from out in the valley itself, there could be no mistaking the fact that the running horses were moving further away; but surely it must be only a matter of minutes before the men realized that the single rider was no longer ahead of them. Nonetheless, Crown first poured all of the remaining water from his canteen into his hat, and for what it was worth, gave it to the horse. Again he thought that this respite he had bought would likely be one of only short duration and that he must therefore waste no time in emerging from this place out into the valley once again, and he chose to do so by walking out of the stygian shadows into the wash of moonlight, leading the bay.

For a moment or two he stood looking towards the head of the valley, all sounds from the riders now having died away; the night had fallen quiet. Crown's first thought was that they had come to a halt, seeing that their quarry was no longer ahead of them, and that at any moment they might come hastening back in his direction. Accordingly, he got into the saddle once again and prepared to make his way out of the valley which, large though it was, he had come to regard as a possible trap.

On the night air the deep gunshots sounded; one, two-three . . . four. Crown halted, turned the horse, listening, not hopeful of seeing anything at the distance indicated by the sound of the shots. However, he was surprised to discern, away up there, a glimmering of light. Judging distances was never an easy matter at night, but as far as he could estimate, the small brightness — and he was convinced that it was not a campfire — would be perhaps a mile away. Another gunshot; and another. Crown was undecided. This was his opportunity, one that might not easily come again, to slip away out of the valley and choose freely where he would go next; yet knowing the stripe of men his pursuers had been, and recalling the scenes at the lone wagon, Crown felt a tug of concern for whoever it might be up there in the night, beset as he believed, by the men whom he had given the slip. It had been his own flight that had brought them riding into this remote place.

Almost a mile from where he had begun, he could see quite clearly in the moonlight, a homestead with a barn and several smaller outbuildings and all around it, squares of cultivated ground, though there seemed to be little crop growth in evidence now. He could hear distinctly the whooping of riders apparently circling the place and there was still an occasional gunshot and he could see the fire-stabs from pistols being blasted into the air. It looked and sounded for all the world like a bunch of drunken cowboys hoorawing along the main street of some cowtown. As far as he could make out there was no gunfire coming from the homestead. It was not until he heard yet another shot from the circling riders and this time also heard the sound of glass smashing, that Crown decided to take a hand. He had only just begun to move forward, however, when he heard one of the men call.

"They're comin' out!" and Crown believed he saw someone in light clothing emerge onto a porch at the back of the house. Whatever lamps had been on earlier, whose glimmering he had seen from afar, they were now turned low and it was difficult to make out whether it was a man or a woman standing there, or whether or not they were armed, for the porch itself was deeply shadowed. The mounted men who had been circling and yelling and shooting had now ridden into the small, moon-washed yard and Crown, as he drew nearer at a walk and still as yet unseen by them, heard one of them say loudly:

"Where is the bastard? Send 'im out here!"

Crown had no doubt that it was he they were asking about and at once felt justified in having come to discover the reason for the shooting.

A female's voice called back to them but Crown could not catch what was said; but that at once became clear when the man who had first spoke said:

"Lyin' to protect him'll on'y buy yuh real trouble!"

That did it for Crown. He started the horse forward and they did not hear him until he was a matter of eighty feet from them and then they sprang their horses apart, wheeling them, and in the light of the moon Crown could easily pick out the moustached man, who now drew down on him, and there was a flash and a report as he fired at Crown; but the horse of the man shooting had been moving and the slug went well astray. And all three horses near the house twisted and plunged, whickering, as Crown levelled his long pistol and in a start of flame and a blaze of sound, shot at the moustached man and hit him hard so that his arms went wide and his body lifted and he fell from the unsettled horse and disappeared down into shadows. Somebody else fired at Crown but to no result, and Crown, having swung down from the saddle, shot again but did not believe he had hit either of them. The moustached man seemed somehow to have come up off the ground and grabbed hold of a stirrup and then all three were retreating in some confusion, one other man leaning down trying to help the one hanging onto the horse, all moving, calling out urgently to each other. Crown then noticed that whoever it was — the woman — who had been on the porch, had vanished. The two mounted men and the man struggling to mount had now passed out of the whiteness of the yard to somewhere beyond the bulking barn. Because they were out of his view he preferred to practice caution in following them up too closely, having no desire to ride in, clearly visible, on top of waiting guns, so instead walked the horse nearer to the house, and in sharp shadows there, dismounted. He could hear their raised voices, though further off now, and presently all fell quiet; then there was the sound of horses moving away, blowing, and then a man cried out as though in pain, and that was all.

The moon sailed on and Crown stood quietly in the night. From the homestead, a place now completely dark, there came no sound. He hitched the bay to a rail of the porch.

"Hullo!" called Crown, but though

he waited several minutes he drew no response. "They've gone!" he called, but again to no avail. "I mean you no harm," Crown said, and to his surprise, for he had not called but spoken it, a girl's voice, obviously from just on the other side of the door, asked:

"Who are you?"

"My name is James Crown. Those men . . . it was me they were looking for. If it hadn't been for me they might not have come into this valley at all."

Silence for a time, then:

"How do you know they have gone?"

"They've gone. I know."

"Then you can go too, now."

"I want to allow more time for them to get well clear. Then I'll go."

"I don't — you're not wanted here! You've no business with us."

"I know it. But the horse at least needs a breather. They'd given us a good run earlier, but I'd give them the slip."

"A man was shot and fell. Is he dead?"

"No. Gone with them, wherever they've gone."

"What brought you here, if you had got away from them?"

"I heard the gunshots. Then I heard a window go."

"Stay away from it. I'll shoot if you come near it."

"I don't even know which one it was." He did not believe, now that she had anything to shoot with. He repeated: "I mean you no harm."

"I won't open the door to you."

"I won't try to come in. But I could use some rest for an hour or two. In your barn maybe."

A prolonged pause followed; so long that he thought she must have gone away. And then she said:

"Don't come near the house again."

He read that as the permit to bunk in the barn, so he made plenty of noise, unhitching the horse, slapping it gently and talking to it, then led it away across the yard. Just before he left, however, he thought he heard voices from inside the house. When he pulled one of the barn's tall doors open he realized that another horse was already inside, for he heard it stamping and blowing.

"Easy there!" said Crown; but before leading his own horse in, he struck a match and held it up and in the quick flare of it saw that a farm horse, a mare, stood in one of two stalls on the far side of the barn. He caught sight, too, of an oil lamp hanging from a beam. A few moments later the lamp was beginning to glow and he hung it back up on its rusty hook.

There was feed in here for the horse and, to his amazement, a trough with some water in it. Cupping his hands he scooped some up, sniffed it, tasted it with his tongue, discovered it was reasonably fresh though warm, and held some in his mouth before swallowing it. The bay took to it readily while Crown hefted the saddle off, removed bedroll, lariat and canteen. From its scabbard he withdrew his rifle and leaned it against the saddle. Water.

He wondered how the hell they had come by it. Another look at the mare, standing peacefully, confirmed that it was in better shape than most animals he had come across in recent weeks. And not only water but good-tasting water, somewhat better than he had had in his canteen. Since the parching seasons had settled across the land he had heard stories of many people who had fallen sick through having drunk the last of sedimented water from their wells, and they had made him very cautious. The horse seen to, he went out into the bright yard and stood for a while quite still, listening for any sounds in the night, but none came to him. The homestead, too, stood dark and quiet. Crown turned and went back into the barn. After he had gone a curtain moved, fell back into place.

5

WHEN the eastern sky had become streaked with light, Crown rose and went to look out from the doorway of the barn. The sun was not yet up but the atmosphere was warm, though as yet the dry, choking wind had not come up. Now he could make an appraisal of the other buildings around the yard, all of them dried and heat-curled, greyish in colour, blown grit having worn away at them; and the blocks of land which once must have borne crops were for the most part brown and dried up. Altogether the scene which lay before him was one of forlorn waste, rough, dried grass standing along the edges of the buildings, nothing stirring except a thin finger of smoke from the stone chimney.

He walked slowly out into the yard

and, nearing its middle, the hard surface cut about in places by the horses that had been there hours earlier, he could see a scattering of dark droplets where the moustached man had been hit; and there was another smear of blood across the ground, marking the place where he had been hanging onto the moving horse.

Crown, responding to an uneasy feeling he had, glanced at the house and realized that he was being observed, and even as he became aware of it, a curtain dropped back into place. He allowed his attention to shift then, towards the baking shapes of the Flinter Hills and thought that the sooner he started the sooner he would cross them. He moved away towards the barn but had taken only a couple of paces when he heard the porch door open. Though he looked back, by the time he did so it was closing again.

Crown stopped, still looking. The door remained closed but there was something on the porch. Unhurriedly

he made his way across and went up
the two stout wooden steps and lifted
the clean blue and white checkered
cloth which had been used to cover
a metal plate containing two slabs of
bacon, a chunk of brownish bread
and knife and fork; and next to it
was a tin mug of steaming coffee.
Without a word he gathered it up and
walked across to the barn and went
in. Crown was hungry and polished
it off in quick time and, hunkered
down on the straw-littered floor, sipped
the rich coffee gratefully. It was quite
unexpected but he was not about to
question it, merely be thankful for it.
But he could not help thinking about
the coffee in particular. It meant that
they had more water in the house.
Crown had not yet saddled the bay
but spent a few minutes assembling
his belongings preparatory to doing so.
By the time he had finished this, and
carrying the plate and mug and utensils
in one hand, walked outside again,
the sun had reached burning fingers

between the yard buildings and a faint warm breeze was already stirring dust.

Up on the porch he knocked on the door, waited. Presently the young woman's voice said:

"Just leave them there."

"I'm obliged to you for the breakfast," said Crown, "an' I want to be on my way right soon. My canteen's empty though. Do you have any water to spare? If the answer is no, then that's it, I'll move on." And he repeated what he had said in darkness. You've nothing to fear from me."

When there was no response he placed the mug and other utensils on it down on the porch and went down the steps. Going back across the yard he was already trying to calculate how long it would take him to get across the Flinters, and trying to visualize what prospect might await him on the other side. He had almost reached the barn when he again heard the house door open, but believing that the girl would simply be retrieving the breakfast things he did not at first glance around; but just as he was entering the barn, he did, and was surprised to see her still standing on the porch watching him, the plate and mug on the boards at her feet. Crown paused, unsure what he ought to do but thought then that he had nothing to lose and began to walk back slowly across the yard. She did not move. As he came nearer he was able to see her clearly and was surprised how youthful she was; no more than eighteen at a guess, a little more than average height, with narrow shoulders and a small, pinched-in waist. She had a heart-shaped face, a short straight nose and full lips. Her hair, pulled back at her neck and coiled there and secured with a dark ribbon, was the colour of wheat, and as he came to the steps of the porch and stopped, Crown could see that the eyes looking back at him were of a delft blue colour, large and clear and compelling. She was wearing a workday dress, not new but very clean, blue and white, and over it a vari-coloured patchwork apron. Her very slim, long-fingered hands were clasped at her midriff, yet he sensed the tension in her. Crown touched the brim of his hat.

"I'm real sorry I caused them to come here," he said, "last night. I'd shaken them near the head of the valley, about a mile from here. They rode on. It was then that I heard the firing."

"It can't be helped," the girl said in a low, clear voice. "It's done now." Then: "Who were they? Why were they looking for you?"

He shrugged. "It could have been for the small amount of water I had at the time. That's how it started out anyway. But I doubt it. They were strangers to me. I rode into their camp; but I had to face them down an' that seemed to rub them the wrong way." She stared at him unsmilingly. "I'm headed across the Flinters," he said, "that was why I asked for the water."

She seemed to be weighing the

matter in her mind, her eyes shifting in one direction then another, before returning to the man in the yard below her, as though she had been wishing for someone to refer to, to take the decision. Finally she said:

"There is some water. There will be enough for your canteen and enough for the horse to be well watered before you leave."

"I can't tell you how much of a relief it is to hear that," said Crown.

She was still uncomfortable with him though, he could tell. There was no softening of her expression, no withdrawal of the mistrust in her eyes. Whatever else she might have said to him concerning the water, however, had to wait. From somewhere inside the house came a faint call and name that sounded like Rebecca. The girl stepped back half a pace, turned her head, then looked again at Crown. Clearly she was undecided what to do about him.

"Don't come any further, mister,"

she said. "Wait." She gave him a last, long look, then her skirts whipped as she turned and went quickly back inside.

Crown thrust big hands into his belt and wandered away from the porch to wait for her to come out again. The sun was now up and beginning to burn and the dry wind had strengthened, bowling small clouds of dust across the ground, setting clumps of dry grass moving stiffly. Water, thought Crown. It seemed almost too good to be true, but what the wagoner, Sellers, had said came back to him, of the unpredictability of underground streams, particularly close in to the hills. With this new hope, he figured that, having provided the horse with whatever water it needed, and gaining a full canteen as well, then by this same time tomorrow he should not only be across the Flinters, but well on his way to Saffron.

He had not heard her come out again

69

so was not even aware of her until she spoke.

"There's a pail in the barn. Fetch it and your canteen." He nodded, crossed to the barn and brought them. When he approached the porch she reached out a slim arm as soon as he set foot on the lower step. "I'll get it." She took the wooden pail from him, and even the weight of it, empty, pulled her arm down. "Put the canteen on the porch. I'll fill that next." He did so. After she had gone inside he heard the sound of a pump handle being worked, and water slopping.

It was all she could manage, using both hands, to get the filled pail out onto the porch. Crown lifted it easily and walked to the barn and emptied it into the trough, where both the bay and the mare moved to it at once. Back at the porch, he remarked:

"That's real sweet water, ma-am."

She took the pail in and filled it again. When she dumped it down she said:

"Before this house was raised, my pa had men down from Calder or somewhere, and they made a good, deep well. But now I don't know how long it will last."

While he made his second journey to the barn she filled his canteen and when he returned it was on the porch along with a large tumbler of water. Crown drank that thankfully. He could see that she was still regarding him warily, but he said:

"There are men roaming all through the territory like those who were here last night, and worse. Have you got no weapon here? No firearm?"

Now there could be no doubting the suspicion in the light blue eyes studying him, yet she said:

"There's a rifle that was my pa's, but it doesn't work any more."

"Will you let me see it?"

She hesitated only a moment before going inside the house. Again he heard a low murmuring of voices but she came out again soon carrying a long rifle which seemed too heavy for her. Crown took it from her, inspected it, but saw at once that the trigger mechanism was broken.

"I'd have to strip it to be certain, but I reckon a gunsmith is what this one needs. I've handled plenty of weapons but I'm not a gunsmith." He propped it on the porch. "Can *you* handle such a weapon?"

"I could fire it from a rest," the girl said. "My pa showed me how; and how to keep the butt snug into the shoulder and to breathe up through the target."

Crown nodded. While she watched him he strode away across the yard to the barn and presently returned carrying his own rifle and a small wax-board box of ammunition. He held the rifle out to her and, doubtfully, she took it. It was half the weight and not nearly as long as the one she had fetched out.

"It feeds through that spring slot," Crown said, pointing. "It's got a full magazine and you work this lever, underneath, to bring each fresh load into the chamber. Keep it by you day an' night."

A small flush had come into her cheeks.

"I can't. It's yours, worth a lot of money. And what about you, moving through the territory? It could save your life."

Crown tapped the canteen. "You just did that. Right now, it's worth ten rifles."

"I can't — "

You must. And if you'll show me the window the bullet went through I'll see what can be done with it, to keep the blown grit out."

She was still not sure. But the other, very faint voice from somewhere inside the house came again. The girl, taking the rifle with her, turned.

"This way." He followed her in. "Through there." Ahead of him was a small square room with an earth floor, damp from the pumping of water, that it was necessary to step down into. It was here indeed that the water pipe came up, the heavy wood and brass pump handle above it. In the far wall was a small unshuttered window in which the bullet had not only punched a spider-cracked hole, but had also taken out a corner-piece of the glass. The girl had not preceded him into the pumphouse but had gone to the left through a door into the kitchen which had a plank floor. Crown saw that in the small, dim annex-room where he stood, broken glass had been carefully brushed into a corner. He was still examining the damaged window when the girl came back. She did not have the rifle now. "My mother," she said. "She's ill."

"Is she bad?"

"She's dying." It was a bald statement of fact, something that obviously the girl had had to face up to and it told Crown as plainly as anything could that there was no hope, and she knew it.

"I'm sorry." Then he said: "Has a

doctor seen her?"

"He came for the last time weeks ago. From Albertine; but he said he was leaving there. He did bring some things he said might help. They didn't. There's nothing more to be done."

Suddenly Crown felt that his concerns about water and his own plans for survival now seemed paltry.

"Is there no-one else here?"

"My pa you mean? No, he's been dead for years." She looked at the window. "I'd thought of knocking all the glass out and putting some wood across it, but it helps to have daylight in here."

Crown nodded. "Maybe some cloth could be forced in there, and be enough to keep the grit out."

She brought some, and Crown, reaching up easily, spent a few minutes wedging it into the gap, making sure it was firm and would not readily dislodge. He indicated the pump.

"Has the water been flowing good, all through?"

"Not always. Some days there's a better flow than others; but what has come up has been clear, tasted good. But there's nowhere near enough for crops."

"Where did that water come from, before the drought?"

"There's a creek runs down a ravine, off the Cimrie, and cuts right down through this valley, along the other side. It crosses about where our north field was and pa had cut channels off it for irrigation. If you came up the valley on the opposite side you wouldn't have had to cross the bed of it. Until two seasons back there was always plenty of water."

Crown nodded sombrely. "All across the flats," he said, "all the way down from Reever's, anywhere near to the bed of the Cimrie itself, there are the whitening bones of dead cattle." He looked squarely at her. You've got water maybe for some while, but you gave me some of your food as well. How will you survive?"

There were some animals we raised for meat. The bacon is about all done, but there's other salted meat, plenty, and some jars of preserves." It was all said in a matter-of-fact way and he realized that, young through she undoubtedly was, the way of life out here in this remote valley had taught her the ways of survival, to make do, not give in, and he felt a warmth towards her that was unexpected and not easy to explain. But it had come time for him to go.

He had got as far as the door leading to the porch when he was fetched up short by an exclamation from her.

"Look!" She was at the pumphouse window, pointing, and he stepped across quickly. Perhaps a matter of a hundred yards away, on the edge of one of the dried-out, once-cultivated patches of ground, stood a horse with a man on it who appeared to be crouching, maybe ducked away from the dust out there.

"Fetch the rifle," Crown said. "Follow

me outside and wait at the corner of the house. I'll saddle up and ride out to him. If he comes on in and I don't, go back in the house and lock the door. Drop anybody that tries to come in. If you hit him fair and square he won't get up." She had been about to say something but he was already off the porch and jogging across the yard to the barn, the dry wind tugging at his clothing as he went. To the girl, the dusty wind also whipping at her, it might have seemed a long while before he came out of the barn with the saddled bay and swung up, but in fact it was only a very few minutes.

Though the dust blowing across occasionally screened the lone horse and rider out there, apart from tossing its head from time to time the animal had not moved. She watched it and then she watched the big man, Crown, go walking his own horse out towards it, his glance moving left and right, looking for others who might be there, seeing none.

Sixty feet from the standing horse, Crown came to a halt. He could now see that the rider was not crouching but was slumped forward with his head, hatless, down against the animal's neck, and one arm hanging. Though Crown could not entirely see the face there was something familiar about the man; and suddenly he knew who it was. It was the man with the ginger moustache, the man he had hit the night before, and now Crown could see the dried blood from him all down the shoulder and near foreleg of the horse. Crown went forward all the way and looked at him and saw that he was dead.

It was the high, shrill call from the girl that came to him next, enough for him to send the big bay dancing sideways away from the other horse with its dead man, and came up with the long pistol in his hand even as they began shooting at him.

6

THE horse with the dead man on it threw up its head and cantered away, the body slipping further to the left side and looking as though, in death, the moustached man was reaching down for something his fingers could not quite grasp. The horse was blowing and clearly now wanting to be rid of its burden, and after travelling for about a hundred and fifty feet, the body slid right down and bounced soddenly on the rough ground, yet one boot was still caught in a stirrup.

Crown was only peripherally aware of all this, however, for he was now urgently occupied in trying to get himself well out of range, yet without being precisely aware of where the shooters were; though the girl must have seen them from where she was, at the house. He did know that they were in brush some forty yards away to his right; and if either of them — for it was obvious to him that it would be the round-faced, chubby man and the other, whom he had come to think of as Eyebrows — had been reasonable marksmen, using long pistols, probably from a rest, then they ought to have been able to clip him with at least one of the half-dozen slugs they had sprayed in his direction. It seemed to him almost miraculous that the horse had not been struck. When he had opened the range to a little under sixty yards Crown turned the horse and, gun in hand, waited.

Even so, he was unprepared for what happened next. Out of the clump of brush that he had been watching, suddenly appeared the round-faced man mounted on a sleek black and coming at a dead run, raising much dust and yelling something at Crown, and as he came, shooting at him. But the shooting, at the long range at which it began, and done as it was from a running horse, was no better than Crown would have expected from a man who, earlier, and in more favourable circumstances, had failed to nail him. Crown waited, sitting absolutely still, then levelled his own pistol, and at a range of thirty feet, knocked the big man out of the saddle, and the now freed horse went galloping on by, its rider rolling over and over, finally flopping to rest some fifteen feet from where Crown was. That episode had demanded all of Crown's attention and it was only as another sound came that he then saw that Eyebrows, having apparently tried to circle him, stood up amid low brush, pistol raised, in a position across Crown's left shoulder and about forty feet from him. The sound was the lash of a rifle shot, and dust leaped between Crown and Eyebrows, causing the latter to jump back in alarm, the pistol in his hand swinging wide, and Crown, seizing the moment, drew a bead on the man and called:

"Even if you stopped me, she'd open your belly with the next one." Eyebrows let go his pistol. Crown waved towards the house, hoping the girl would interpret it as a signal that the danger was past. To Eyebrows he said: "Well, whatever the hell it was that you thought you wanted to do, it's all to hell an' gone now. Listen to me. Leave that damn' Colt where it is an' get yourself out of this valley an' be glad you're still alive to do it. But before you go, round up their horses an' get those two clowns back up on 'em an' tow 'em out with you. Maybe the one with the moustache is still caught up on his. I've hired on at this place, so if you ever have a mind to ride in again, I'll kill you on sight. You believe that, friend. Now move."

A half hour later Crown was in the yard and the girl was standing there also, still holding Crown's rifle, watching Eyebrows leading his small procession of dead far down the hot valley.

"He'll not come back this time," said Crown, remembering that he had given her the hint of a similar belief only a few hours ago. She merely looked at him, a flat neutrality in her expression and Crown felt a sense almost of shame, reading into that look as plainly as though she had spoken it aloud, her belief that he was now patronizing her. "I told him," Crown added, "that I'd hired on here."

"And do you think he believed you?"

"I have no way of knowing that," he said. He found the open, serious stare of her clear eyes unsettling, as though she could see right through him. Young she might well be, but something had aged her beyond her years; this place no doubt, these circumstances, these seasons of death.

Suddenly she turned her head, listening, then left him abruptly, the dust-whorls spinning by him, to go inside the house, leaving the rifle on the porch. When, after a few minutes, she came to the back door, Crown was still standing where he had been. He could see by her face that something was badly wrong and she could easily read the question in his.

"She's dead. My mother's dead."

★ ★ ★

The girl, Rebecca, had prepared for burial the wax-like, wasted body of the woman who had been her mother, Evelyn Parr. She had wrapped her in clean linen and laid her on the mattress on top of the iron bed in the sparsely-furnished room in which she had slept for most of her adult life and in which, now, with a faint, meaningless cry, a flicker of eyelids and a drawing back of near-colourless lips over teeth, she had died. Crown considered that, at least in her last few years it had not been much of a place to live, though at the instant of departure from life, to whatever might follow, the matter was probably of small concern. Rebecca Parr was pale, dry-eyed, tight-lipped, moving to her necessary tasks without delay, as though she might have rehearsed in her mind a number of times, the demands of this moment.

He said: "I'll make a coffin as best I can," and she looked at him, round-eyed, and nodded.

Crown scoured barn and outbuildings and in one of the latter, little more than a lean-to, on an old flat-deck wagon that seemed not to have been used in years, found some lengths of pine lumber, many curled and grey with age, a few usable, and a box of ginger-rusted steel clouts. In an adjoining shed he found a saw and hammers of various weights, and some heavy gauge staples. He saw that the workable lumber that he had would not be sufficient and, failing to discover any more, took the heaviest of the hammers and banged a couple of planks off the lean-to itself.

After fully two hours of labour in pulsing heat, plagued constantly by blown dust and flies, Crown, stripped to the waist, stood back and surveyed the long box that he had fashioned. It was rough and of a plain oblong shape but sturdily made and was now ready to be taken to the house. The day was well advanced by now. The girl must have been watching him, sensing that he was almost finished, for as he shrugged into his shirt, she came across the yard to where he was, one hand guarding her eyes from the dust. She was calm but still very pale. Crown said:

"Show me where the grave is to be dug and I'll get on with that." He knew that there was an adze and a spade in the same place in which he had found the hammers and the saw. She looked at him, strands of bright hair drifting about her neck, and she shook her head.

"You've done more than enough today. I'll make supper soon. The digging can wait until tomorrow."

"Where, then?"

She turned her head and pointed to where, about fifty yards from the house, there was already a low mound covered by stones.

"Up there, next to my pa." She walked away towards the house, Crown following silently in her wake.

Later, he fed the horses, checked also that water remained in the trough; then, as she stood at a window, gave a sign and she came out and together they carried and manoeuvred the pine box into the house. In the bedroom they set two chairs to support it and Rebecca produced more linen and with that, lined it inside. Then together, with gentleness, as though she might simply be sleeping, lifted the — to Crown — weightless body of Evelyn Parr, whom he had never known in life, and placed it in the coffin. Crown went out and brought in the planks for the top but the girl shook her head.

"Tomorrow."

He nodded, left her alone.

Two hours before sun-up, working

alternately with adze and spade, Crown began the task of digging the grave in flint-hard ground. As the sun fired the homestead yard he paused at her call, for food and coffee, then without delay returned to his aching, bone-jarring task. It was near noon, his torso slick with sweat, and with blown dust raking at him that he climbed out of the trench he had made and set about gathering smooth stones which, afterwards, would be laid thickly over the burial mound. By early afternoon he had nailed the top planks of the coffin into place and together Crown and the girl edged it out of the house and carried it, pushed by the hot wind, to the place that Crown had made ready to receive it. The business of lowering it into the grave, Crown took upon himself, using his lariat, securing it around head and foot, looping the rope over his right shoulder, standing alongside the grave, then relying on his own strength, lowering the coffin down into the ground. He then climbed down and undid the lariat and drew it out with him.

Rebecca, having returned to the house to bring out a very old prayer book, stood now with her skirts pressed against her back by the wind, strands of her hair flying. While Crown stood with her, his hat in his hands before him, she began to read in a clear voice:

"The Lord is my shepherd: therefore can I lack nothing.

He shall feed me in a green pasture; and lead me forth beside the waters of comfort.

He shall convert my soul; and bring me forth in the paths of righteousness, for his Name's sake.

Yea, though I walk through the valley of the shadow of death, I will fear no evil; for thou art with me; thy rod and thy staff comfort me.

Thou shalt prepare a table before me against them that trouble me; thou hast anointed my head with oil, and my cup shall be full.

But thy loving kindness and mercy shall follow me all the days of my life; and I will dwell in the house of the Lord for ever."

It was evening and she had lit a lamp.

"Before they were married," she said, "my mother taught school in Denver, Colorado, then in other, smaller places."

"What brought them to this region, to live off the land?"

"It so happened that they were both from farming stock up in Kansas. Both of them, my mother used to say, felt stifled, enveloped by family; and there were some tensions. I don't know why. They decided to get away, strike out on their own, and eventually came down here. This is where I was born. They would have made it, too, drought or no drought, for they'd paid the bank and lifted their title, but then my pa fell ill. He'd been to Albertine and to Hope, making new deals for produce, and he was still in Hope, loading some farm materials he'd bought there, when he gashed a hand. There was no-one in the town who could treat it properly, so he came on home. My mother did her best, but it got really bad and turned to blood poisoning. After that my mother and I carried on as best we could, but she got sick, and the doctor I fetched from Albertine finally said there was nothing more he could do for her. He left plenty of laudanum. We'd already had one bad, dry season, the creek dry and the crops shrivelling; then this, the second one. And now she's dead. She was a good woman. My pa was a good man. They didn't ask anything of anybody else. I had a happy life here; lonely maybe, but there are plenty who have it worse. It was hard, always, but I had advantages others didn't have in places like this. My mother could teach me as well — better even — than if I had been able to go to school. She gave me that, because there was so much else that neither of them could give me. Love and learning, they gave me. Come with me."

She took the lamp and led Crown through to an adjoining room, and he was astonished to see that, little more than a store-room, it contained books, piles of them; on the floor, on two makeshift tables, on shelves that had been fixed to the walls. He ran his hand over soft calf binding and gilt edging. "My pa told me they almost needed a second wagon coming down here, just to carry her books. My mother said she made certain, in spite of his doubts, that she took her other world along with her wherever they went." Crown thought it the most unexpected sight he had come across in a very long while. But he said.

"What will you do now?"

She led the way back into the kitchen and set the lamp down.

"This piece of land belonged to them. Now it comes to me alone. I want to leave, yet I want to stay, too. Anyway, who would buy such a place as this in times such as these?"

"There won't always be a drought."

"But how long will it be? When will it end? Next season? The one after?"

There could be no answers and she did not expect any from him. He left her, made his way to the barn and prepared his bedroll. There had been no further mention of when he would leave, but he believed it would be the following morning. There was no more he could do here and Rebecca Parr must now make up her own mind what her plans would be. In the short while he had known her he had developed for her a certain respect. And undeniably she was an attractive girl, not yet worn down by the rawness of life in such a place. Vulnerable too, she was, now more than ever before; a young woman alone, remote, owning property, such as it had become, but most importantly, possessing a good well that yielded clear water in this parched, benighted land. He did not, he thought, give one hell of a lot for her chances.

7

CROWN slept very soundly, yet awoke knowing that his awakening had been because of a noise. He moved quickly but when he looked out across the pale dawn yard, saw that he had been too slow in moving, for the horse, a dust-streaked chestnut, was already hitched to the porch rail, and its rider, having dismounted, was up on the porch talking with Rebecca Parr. Crown could see that the visitor was wearing range clothing and was holding his wide-brimmed hat in one hand. It was not possible to see his face but Crown did see now that Rebecca was listening to the man rather than talking with him. Crown buckled his gunbelt on, loosened the big pistol in its holster and walked quietly across the yard; but the visitor heard him coming and turned to watch him. Significantly, Crown saw that as soon as the man on the porch did so, Rebecca Parr withdrew into the house, and he believed that she would immediately go to the rifle. Crown studied the man. He was aged perhaps in his late twenties, a cowboy by the looks of him, leather chaps over his trousers, faded blue shirt, red bandanna, and the stained, high-crowned hat that he was holding. Slung with a shellbelt, he had a Colt holstered high on his right hipbone. His face was deeply tanned and when he smiled his teeth were seen to be startlingly white.

"Mornin'," said Crown, coming to a stop a half-dozen paces short of the porch.

"An' good mornin' friend, to you," the stranger said, exposing his pristine teeth. It was an open, disarming smile, but at the same time Crown was aware that he himself was being carefully examined from boots to hat and back again. The cowboy came down off the porch and extended his hand which Crown grasped briefly. "My handle's Billy Grieve." Crown nodded. So this was Billy Grieve. He had heard of him. Although he had extended his hand readily enough he seemed to have difficulty holding Crown's eyes.

"Jim Crown." If that surprised or even startled the other, he concealed it well; but Crown thought he did detect the merest narrowing of eyes, but only for an instant. And whatever his attire might suggest, and whatever he might have been at some time in the past, Crown thought that it had probably been some while since Grieve had been employed to herd cattle. And his wide smile meant less than nothing. Grieve waved a casual hand.

"This your place, Crown?" Grieve was looking all around him.

"No," said Crown, "but I help around here."

"Help," said Grieve. He rubbed at the tip of his nose with one gloved hand. "Well now. It's just that I wouldn't, on sight, have taken yuh for a — " waving his hand vaguely, "a farmer."

"Looks can be deceiving," said Crown.

"That they can," said Billy Grieve. "That they can." It was clear that he had no intention of leaving immediately, for he hitched one leg up onto the porch rail and began to build a smoke from makings he had produced from a pocket of his shirt. Crown could see that Rebecca Parr had reappeared, though not quite coming into the doorway; and if she had the rifle nearby he could see no sign of it.

"We don't get a lot of visitors out here," said Crown.

The match flared brightly as Billy Grieve lit his quirly, then described a swift, thin-smoking arc as he flicked it away. "I guess yuh don't at that. Not many." Crown began to wonder if Grieve might have met up with Eyebrows towing his dead away and as a consequence know more about what had taken place here than he would feel inclined to reveal. Then Grieve, popping a blue smoke-ring, then another, said: "Yuh must be among the few survivors in this here territory, Crown. Most other places, it's bad. Real bad. Was up in Hope a few days back. Last week. Not too many left in that town now. They do have some water though; just a little. They're not real keen on sharin' it around. Me, I was gonna go up around Albertine like a lot more done, but I cain't see how it woulda been no better there. Not with all them folks goin' in. Besides, I allers found that town to be a pesky, troublesome place. Troublesome." He sniffed, drew on his smoke. "I move around a lot."

"I reckon I've heard of you," said Crown.

Grieve's face split in another dazzling smile but still he did not look at Crown directly.

"I wouldn't be surprised," he said. But he was not smiling and was looking at his boots when he said: "I reckon I heard o' you, too, Crown."

"I wouldn't be surprised," said Crown.

Rebecca Parr, listening, saw that, diffident or not, this man was showing no inclination to leave and thought also that she sensed a tension growing between him and Crown. She came into the doorway and Crown could read nothing in her expression as she said:

"There's hot biscuits and coffee if you've a mind to eat."

"Well now," said Grieve, slapping his knee, "if that ain't real neighbourly. Indeed, real neighbourly." He dropped the remnant of his smoke onto the porch and squashed it with the toe of a boot, then hitched himself off the rail and preceded Crown through into the kitchen, his gaze probing the pumphouse as he went by.

Seated at a table that was covered with a crisply clean green and white checkered cloth, he fell to the meal, as did Crown, while Rebecca Parr moved about at her stove, taking no part in the conversation. But Billy Grieve's eyes constantly flicked back to watch the girl. Then Crown asked:

"What is it exactly that you consider to be troublesome in Albertine?"

It was not the kind of question he would ordinarily have asked of a stranger but he wanted to distract this one, and besides, he had him pegged as a boaster and probably a liar.

"Huh?" At first Grieve looked almost startled, then smiled broadly. "Oh that," he said. "Yeah, I did say that. Well, there was some aggravation there some while back. Feller named Stalker. Card man, Stalker, come from El Paso so they do say. But he moved around a lot."

"Like yourself," said Crown. Now he recalled that Billy Grieve had shot to death — and it seemed that it had been in Albertine — a professional gambler; shot him because of some old score that had become a burr under Billy's saddle.

"That's it," Grieve nodded. "Funny thing was," he went on, "he didn't right off recall me, Stalker didn't. I reckon he give the fast shuffle to so many folks he couldn't no more put faces to half of 'em. Well, I come across him, dealin', up, like I say, in Albertine; place called Rorke's. Well, I shore give him a hint or two, quiet like, an' still he don't tumble, 'til another feller in there calls out to me an' calls me Billy, an' finally, this Stalker, he says: 'Are you Billy Grieve?' an' I says 'That's right, I'm him. I'm William C. Grieve an' I'm as mean as dogshit an' I'm here to blow yore Goddamn' face into New Mexico' an' then by Gawd it was all on an' hootin' I kin tell yuh!" Grieve finished his coffee and set the cup down. "An well, a man does some things that are loco an' mebbe some bad things, but not all bad an' not all loco. There's some good parts in between."

Crown studied him, but Grieve would look anywhere but at him.

Crown thought that he could not immediately perceive many good parts in Billy Grieve and this indeed seemed to fit all that he heard about him in one place and another. For example, by Crown's recollection, derived from what Crown considered to be impeccable sources, Stalker had been shot in the back. And what he knew of Grieve fitted what he knew of men just like him, garrulous, shifty, their eyes not wanting to look at another man directly. Shifty and dangerous, more particularly if the other man's back was turned. He wanted to see Grieve to hell and gone from here for he had also noticed the way the man's eyes had followed every move of the girl, lingering on the way her dress stretched tightly across her narrow back as she bent forward, on the curve of her delicate neck, the fair fuzz on her small, sunbrowned arms; a very pretty young girl, slim as a wand, a feast for the eyes of a man such as Billy Grieve. The girl must have noticed too, but she gave no indication that she had, clearing away dishes, preparing to wash them up; and that was the cue that Billy Grieve had been waiting for.

"Cain't help but notice," he remarked, off-hand, looking at the girl's back rather than at Crown, "yuh do seem to have some water here. Now, that's unusual."

She looked around at him and he savoured the colour of her eyes.

"We do have some," she said, "but there's no telling how long it will last."

Grieve nodded readily. "Just so. Just so," he said. "Nobody knows when that might happen. But I must admit yuh're right fortunate."

"If it's a matter of some for your canteen," she said, "we can manage that."

"More'n generous," said Grieve, but he still made no move to get up; rather, he raked another chair around with the toe of a boot and even with the spur on the boot, succeeded in resting a heel on it. "Different from them up in Hope.

What they did have was all for them. No open-handed generosity there. And there ain't no trust no more. It's as bad as the old days ever was." He glanced towards Crown but his eyes as quickly slid away and his attention settled on the girl again. "Folks wouldn't leave other folks be, back then, neither."

He shook his head as though to free it of distasteful memories. "Good friends gone, through no trust. I mean, for one thing, here we was all gone to Arizona, me an' ol' Buzzard Crane an' Garney Apley, all settin' in on a game o' stud, back of a feed an' grain in Gila Bend an' nobody the wiser so we thought; an' who should bob up large as life an' twice as ornery but that feller Earp. The real big 'un; Wyatt. He come to the back winder an' he called out fer ol' Buzzard to git his ass out there all on account o' some misunderstandin' in Tombstone, a good year gone. Turns out a bastard we all of us knowed had seen us a — comin' an' lit out an' found Earp, who happened to be in the parts an' pissed in his pocket with it, an' so here he was outside an' shoutin' the odds. Buzzard, now, he didn't cotton to walkin' out there to where he knowed that Earp bastard was, so he tippy-toed out front an' some Fancy Dan that Earp had brung with him, he blowed Buzzard's lamp out right there in the street. Nope, cain't trust no bastard nowhere no-how." He shot a look at Crown.

"Yuh know that Earp?"

"We've met," said Crown. He did not think all that much of Earp and his grandstanding bully-boys, once of Tombstone, but he did not see fit to enlighten Billy Grieve on the matter.

"So that," said Grieve, examining his propped-up boot, "was the plumb finish of ol' Buzzard Crane. A good friend to ride along with, was Buzzard."

Rebecca went out of the room to some other part of the house.

"Crane was a useless bag of shit," said Crown quietly, "an' so was Apley."

Billy Grieve blinked his shifty little eyes, still concentrating on the boot that was propped up on the other chair, but a flush mounting in his face. Crown waited expectantly but Grieve did not look at him. Crown stood up. With one foot swinging hard he kicked the chair away against the wall and Grieve's foot fell to the floor and he all but spilled off the chair he was sitting on.

"Out," Crown said. "Up an' out. Now." Grieve came to his feet, his face gone white and his eyes slitted and there was no vestige of a smile now. Rebecca came back into the kitchen to find out what had caused the sudden noise. "Stay clear of him, Rebecca," Crown said. "Billy Grieve, here, has finished his breakfast, for which he is obliged to you, and has finished all his talking as well, an' now he's leaving."

Facing Crown, glance going away, coming back, Billy Grieve was breathing deeply. Then, as though in some strange way he was recalling a pattern of behaviour for just such a moment, pulled back his lips and smiled whitely.

"Now easy, friend. Ain't no call to go gittin' all het up, as I see it."

"You were offered water for your canteen," said Crown in a low voice. "If it was left up to me you'd get something a little less fresh; but it's not up to me. Now, accept the lady's good offer an' then get mounted."

Billy Grieve tried to go on smiling but it did not work any more and his face was bleak as he went out of the house. Crown following, and got the canteen off his horse. Crown, taking it, shook it and felt that there was very little in it. Without taking his eyes off Grieve he held it out and it was taken by Rebecca who, Crown heard, went into the pump-house. Crown then told Grieve to lead his horse across to the barn where he would find a trough with some water in it, and as Grieve did so, Crown followed. He knew enough about Billy Grieve to realize he must not take his attention off him and certainly not turn his back on him.

The horse watered, Grieve led it back to the porch, where Rebecca held out the replenished canteen to him.

"My gratitude, ma'am," said Grieve, "an' may we meet ag'in."

"I think that's unlikely," said Crown.

Grieve swung up into his saddle; he even managed one of his smiles.

"Aw, it's a small world," he said. "Yuh never do know what's gonna come next."

Both of them, standing in the shade and shelter of the house — for the wind had again risen — watched horse and rider moving steadily away down the valley, the individual shapes of both eventually merging and beginning to dance in waves of heat and be obscured from time to time by clumps of brush or jutting rocks or by curtains of white dust.

"He'll survive, won't he, Billy Grieve?" It was hardly a question at all that she posed.

"Oh yes. Whoever else goes down,

Billy's bones won't be among those bleaching in the sun when this is all over. The Billy Grieves of this world always manage to get by, one way or another."

"It might sound odd," she said, "but in the end he frightened me more than the other men did; the ones who were shooting. It was when he smiled that he gave me a feeling of fear such as I've never known before."

"There's good reason," Crown said. "Billy Grieve is more dangerous than those three all rolled into one."

After a short pause, while they continued watching the distant horse and rider become no more than a single dark speck that now hung upon the very edge of vision, she said:

"Was I foolish to offer him the water?"

"No," said Crown at once, "for Billy is no fool. Here we were, survivors, whether or not he'd even come across the trough in the barn and the two well-kept horses; here we were, getting by, looking well nourished; and with what he might have taken to be dampness in the air, from a pumphouse, perhaps, seconds after the porch door was opened — an' you had no real choice other than to open it. No, you weren't foolish to offer water. Maybe, if there was foolishness done, it was by me, putting the hard word on Billy; but I'd got the feeling he'd made his own decision to stay right where the water was."

Rebecca looked at him and when she again looked down the valley she could no longer find the lone horseman. They turned away but for a minute or two did not move from the shade of the house.

"He hasn't gone for good though, Billy, has he?"

Crown thought about it, looked and saw that her clear-eyed expression was calm, and what she had said in her low voice, was a single statement of something perceived. He calculated that from the time of his first glimpse of this slim girl to this moment, perhaps sixty hours had elapsed, and though they had been complete strangers, and she at first most apprehensive of him, events and circumstances had dictated that they share times of danger and a kind of intimacy which made that small number of hours meaningless. Surely he had known Rebecca for a longer time than that.

"No, he hasn't gone for good."

"Water. He'll come back to where he knows the water is." Why should Crown sense something more in her words by the way she spoke them? Yet he did; a kind of defensiveness, as though even Rebecca, in the plain, commonsense way she usually had, wanted to assure herself that there was nothing more, that she was not deluding herself, so left it open for Crown to comment upon. Crown looked at her, at the soft, delicate beauty which she herself seemed to be almost unaware of.

"He'll come back to where the water

is an' he'll come back to where you are. He wants both an' he means to have both." The very faintest trace of colour came into her face. "But you'll have the rifle," Crown said, "and unless, on his way here, he did meet Eyebrows on his way out, he won't know about the rifle. After I've gone, what you must do is follow a careful routine. Never vary it. Always, day an' night, assume that this place is being watched, because sometime, it will be. By Billy. Each morning, go to each window to turn an' study the lay of the land carefully before you open a door. Wait for full daylight, but not until the sun's high an' the wind has fetched the dust up. Be certain that no-one is close by, out there. When you do go outside make sure that the other door is still locked and the windows are all secured. Lock the porch door behind you so nobody can slip inside while you're gone an' be waiting for you. Take the rifle with you an' check the barn an' every other outbuilding. When you take water over to the trough, make several trips, each with a small, manageable amount in the pail so you can carry the rifle in your other hand. There was no rifle on Billy Grieve's horse, so he won't be able to put a bullet in your leg from long range. He would have to come in close to get a shot — an' he wouldn't want to shoot to kill, right off — an' that gives you an edge, an' that's what you have to have over people like him."

She listened to him, never taking her clear gaze from his face as he was speaking. "Do that," Crown said, "an' you'll have a better than even chance of outsmarting Billy Grieve."

They moved away then, she into the house to prepare some food for Crown to take with him, he to gather his belongings together and saddle the horse. First though, he replenished the trough generously so that it would be some little while before Rebecca would need to do so, particularly as only the mare would remain in the barn; because that, Crown considered, topping up the trough, would be the single most vulnerable act she would have to carry out, her times of greatest danger, when she would have to cross the yard with both pail and rifle. He had stood stroking the neck of the horse, allowing it to drink. Now he moved to pick up his saddle blanket, preparatory to putting it in place, when he became aware that she was standing in the doorway of the barn. At first glance, in her deep blue dress, with her thick, straw-coloured hair bunched at her small neck and tied there with a ribbon of blue velvet, she looked more like some shy child who had strayed in, and the sight of her so, caught him unawares.

"How long do you believe it will be before he comes back?"

Crown himself had thought about that, trying to estimate it, but Grieve was a tricky customer and you could never be sure.

"I can't say; but I think it will be a

matter of days. No longer."

She looked at the straw-littered dirt floor of the barn, then up at Crown again.

"I have no right to ask this," she said, "but might you wait for those few days at least? Then, if there's still no sign of him, perhaps he won't come back."

Crown had seen enough of her during these past hours to acknowledge the probable cost to her of asking it of him; for there was, he had observed, in her bearing, in the direct way that she looked and spoke, a pride which could not be mistaken. The recent circumstances of her existence had demanded that this girl of eighteen become more self-reliant than many another female elsewhere, twice her age, yet he had to admit that, in spite of this, as he saw her before him, she was not a woman in her thirties but a girl who was not so many years beyond her childhood and that, even though events had thrust heavy responsibilities so early upon her, she remained that very young woman. Yet he had no desire to wound her pride in dwelling over the request that in truth she would not have wished to make. Instead, when he replied, he simply expressed again some of the thoughts which had indeed come to trouble him about Billy Grieve, and the admission of which, to some extent might keep Rebecca's pride unbruised.

"I said earlier that I had some part in this. I have some guilt over Billy Grieve."

"Guilt?"

Crown moved away a step as the big bay nudged against him.

Yeah. I got hold of the notion that he meant to stay. Now, he might have taken his own sweet time about it, but finally, he might have moved on, unasked."

"Might?"

Crown shrugged. "We have to see it as a possibility. As it was, I took away that option when I came hard down on him. Whichever way you look at it, it wasn't my place to do it, wasn't my house and the water here doesn't belong to me. Maybe all I did was make quite sure that Grieve does come back. Now here I am gettin' ready to ride out an' leave you, rifle or no rifle, with the consequences of that, if there are going to be some."

He could not truly read the effect of what he had said had on her but thought, though perhaps it was really because he wished to do so, that a certain warmth came into the way she looked back at him.

"If I had objected to the way you handled him in our — my house," she said in a not-quite-steady voice, "I would have told you before this."

He nodded. "I guess so. But hearing it said relieves my mind somewhat."

"You do believe he will come back here?"

"Let's say I don't believe it's in his nature, from all I've heard about him, to let it lie. Like his gambling man

118

in Albertine, Grieve won't feel right until, somehow, he's squared matters with me. And with you."

"We watched him fade from sight, but out here in this kind of country, I suppose that means very little."

"I know it. Maybe even as we stand here he's holed up not far away. If I was to leave here now he might take a crack at me, if he could get close in for a back-shot; but I'd be inclined to think he'd let me get well clear, no doubt to track me later, an' he'd come on in here first." He did not need to spell out for her the inferences in that. "At some stage, in some way, probably by not pushing things, he'd catch you when the rifle was out of your reach."

"What will you do, then?"

He was to some degree unsure himself, at least concerning immediate moves, but said: "I could ride away late in the afternoon as though just drifting on from here, but come back under cover of dark. It might — just might — be enough to lure him in, if

119

he *is* out there. But I don't fancy that. Too much depends on trying to guess what a man like Grieve will do, too much rides on the timing. Or I could scout the whole valley, try to flush him out; or prove that he isn't there. That's what I feel would be a better move." He stood before her, looking down. "But either way, now that I know what your thoughts are, I'm not about to leave this place until I'm certain that the danger's past."

She did not answer but on impulse stretched up on her toes, her long, light fingers taking hold of his arms for a moment, and brushed her fresh lips against his cheek, and then in a whirl of skirts, colour pinking her cheeks, fled from the barn.

★ ★ ★

Without haste, but constantly alert, Crown had ridden to the narrowing end of the valley then back along the length of it, passing fifty yards from the buildings, returning Rebecca's wave, then continued on, following approximately the line he had been on when approaching the Parr farm on that first night. He passed the rocky bluff behind which he had taken refuge and then, acting out of prudence, returned to it to make quite sure that the blind clearing was now unoccupied.

Once out of the valley he swung to his left and walked the bay on until he found a place from which he believed it would be possible to climb to higher ground, and began to do so, until the valley itself lay just out of sight somewhere down to his left. He allowed the horse to pick its way between upthrusts of rock, scrappy brush and wind-stunted trees until he judged that he could, by going afoot, reach a vantage point from which he might look down upon the whole long sweep of the valley that he had recently left. He dismounted and hitched the horse to an arm of brush.

Descending to the kind of place that

he sought proved less easy than he had imagined, however, and from time to time it was all he could do to keep his balance and prevent himself sliding down in an uncontrolled plunge among loose stones. But at length, sweating freely from the effort and with white dust clinging to the sweat, he was able to hunker down and see, laid out below him, the valley. Though a good way from where he was, the Parr land stood out, the homestead, barn and other buildings and the once-cultivated blocks surrounding them, now grey and brown and dusty, divested of life; and beyond the farthest of them, where the country again became broken and clumped with brush and strewn with rocks, could see the area to which he had been drawn by the presence of the dead horseman, and had been shot at, and had then killed the round-faced man; and though the valley was filmed with blowing dust, he could also see, as a chalky line, the dried-up creek that once had found its way out of the lumpy hills, all the way from the Cimrie River and now, in this valley, stretched the length of it, nearer to the farther side. And he could see, too, the irrigation channels that Rebecca Parr had spoken of but which were now not easily distinguished, having become choked with wind-blown, dry silt and stunted brush.

Crown could imagine, though, how this place might have looked in better times when water was plentiful, the valley and its flanking hills green and bursting with life, the Parrs' crops standing splendidly in their fields. What a wonderful place it must have been to live, to spend a childhood. Unbidden, the girl's heart-shaped face came back. Impatiently he shrugged it away and set about scrutinizing the valley with slow deliberation. How obvious it was, from here, that there existed down there so many places in which a cunning, patient man could hide himself, bide his time, wait Crown out, wait for the opportunity to close in on the girl.

Yet after almost half an hour engaged in this unhurried scrutiny, Crown came to the belief that Grieve was not in the valley. Of course, Crown could not be absolutely sure but he did feel reasonably so. But out of the valley or not, Crown was still convinced that Grieve had not gone far and had certainly not gone for good. Wherever he might be at this moment, his mind would have shaped a single, implacable purpose, for that was the nature of Billy Grieve and although Crown still felt tugs of nagging guilt, those that he had spoken of to Rebecca, he knew, deep down, that Grieve, having in his first few minutes on the Parr place, perceived both salvation and temptation, would have come, anyway.

Crown, even under the wide brim of his hat, cupped his hands and stared out across the hazy valley to the homestead. Once he thought he caught the flutter of movement, as of a blown skirt, but when he concentrated, could see nothing save the whirling dust. The thought, however, prompted him to stretch his stiffened legs and begin the awkward, slow ascent from where he was to where he had hitched the bay. Once there he took a glance or two around to ensure that he was still alone, then remounted, settling into hot leather, and began to go back the way he had come.

He had made up his mind that he would re-enter the valley across on its farther side, search along the general line of the dead creek, circle every clump of brush, probing it with his eyes, watch his back trail and try to make sure, also, that he himself was not being observed from somewhere up on the hills on either side. In the event, over the long course of his entire ride, he discovered nothing at all to excite suspicion; yet when he was done, the farm buildings once more before him, the tensions were still there for Crown, and his belief that Grieve was not far away was unshaken.

★ ★ ★

She did not need to ask the question for she read the story by the shake of his head as he dismounted in the yard.

"Nothing," Crown said. "Not a sign."

"So he *has* gone out of the valley."

Crown shoved his shallow black hat back, revealing a forehead streaked with sweat and dust. "I reckon so. I can't be absolutely certain, but I reckon so."

Clearly she had heard the horse coming before she had confirmed that it was Crown returning and he was gratified to see that she had been carrying the rifle when she had come out on the back porch.

He was relieved to be back yet now felt that his search and surveillance in poor and uncomfortable conditions had not been a completely wasted effort; for he now had a clear picture in his mind of the whole of the big valley and it had yielded at least one idea which he had tucked into the back of his mind. For one of his chief concerns was ammunition. If Grieve did come back and in some way managed to pin them down, he would need to keep careful count of every shot fired.

It was as he was preparing to lead the dusty bay across the yard to the barn that Rebecca said in a slightly embarrassed way, he thought, possibly because of her display of emotion, earlier:

"When you've seen to him there'll be a meal ready. And best fetch your bedroll across. I've got a room ready for you."

He nodded but made no comment, as though it might have been something he had fully expected, and walked the horse away.

8

DAYS went by in toiling hours of unremitting heat and dust, but Billy Grieve did not come. Crown, for his part, was infinitely more comfortable, physically, in his changed sleeping quarters, yet he still felt some discomfort of mind through, even for a short time and for considerations of safety, coming into the house with Rebecca Parr. It was an arrangement, as he knew full well, that in normal circumstances would simply never have been even remotely possible. Abnormal circumstances, however, had compelled them to it, and he gave the young woman all credit for having perceived the practicality of it; and all this was now silently, tacitly accepted.

Nevertheless there were certain protocols to be observed and Crown, surprising himself, became fastidious, as indeed did the girl, in allowing the other absolute privacy, often for long periods of time. Crown did his bathing in an old wooden tub he discovered in one of the outbuildings, carrying his pails of heated water from the house. He would never enter the house without first calling to her or knocking on the porch door, and completely without discussion, little by little, observing and reacting, they established a quiet, respectful, orderly routine that seemed to fit the needs and eased the minds of both.

It seemed to Crown that an age had passed, yet it was only a handful of hours, since he had stood on the dark porch that first night and she had called through the locked door: ' . . . you're not wanted here. You've no business with us.' He smiled slightly at the recollection. And now, through it all, Crown kept reminding her that they could not afford to allow their vigilance to slacken. He himself several times scouted again the areas of brush out beyond the once-worked land, finding nothing. Crown, too, inspected all of the outbuildings, taking mental note of their contents for possible future use; and he oiled the hinges of the window-shutters all the way around the house.

Searching for some other item, Rebecca one day recovered from an old tin trunk in the room that housed the books, a somewhat battered brass spyglass. One of the lenses was cracked and both were badly scored but the thing still functioned, and with it, Crown and Rebecca spent time, daily, examining the valley and the rusty hills on either hand. It was symbolic of their existence day by day, this careful, tense scrutiny of the surrounding country, in a sense the focus of their own lives. Beyond the concern over Grieve and whether or not he might reappear, there was nothing, no tomorrow, no next week, no further plans of any kind, only the immediacy of watchfulness. Rebecca, thought Crown, seeing sometimes her preoccupation when she did not even realize that he was looking at her, and he not seeing fit to break in on her thoughts, was in fact considering only in the vaguest way what she might do, eventually; but they were indeed nebulous thoughts, ephemeral, no substance to them. She knew that she could not work this farm alone even were the killing drought to come to an end tomorrow; yet there was nowhere else of which she had any real knowledge, except from her books. When she thrust these thoughts aside and returned to immediate concerns, Crown was aware of it by her sudden activity, as though she might be rebuking herself for a lapse, and almost always, looking at him, would say:

"Hand me the glass. I'll watch for a time."

Crown stripped, checked and oiled both the rifle and the long pistol and was gratified to see that Rebecca never let the rifle be far from her reach and never went out of the house without it. Occasionally, perhaps when she believed he was elsewhere, he had seen her raise the weapon to her small shoulder, snugging it well in, and traverse it slowly, sighting it, making herself become accustomed to the shape and feel and weight of it. Crown silently applauded her diligence knowing that, in a bad situation, Rebecca's confidence with the rifle might be all that stood between the both of them and death. However, he was to be given cause to ruminate over that before too much longer.

And still the well remained good. They were careful in that they used only the amount of water genuinely needed, daily, for themselves and for the two horses, but made sure, also, that containers inside the house were full and freshened. As long as drinkable water continued flowing and they remained in control of it, they had a good chance of weathering it through, whether Grieve came or not.

As a strict routine, each day just before sun-up, Crown rose quietly, dressed, armed himself and went out onto the porch, locking the door behind him. Moving as quietly as he could, he checked the inside and the outside of every one of the farm buildings, especially the cavernous barn, most carefully. Then, still afoot, he made a slow, deliberate circuit of the silent homestead to assure himself that no shutter had been tampered with and that there were no boot-scuffs in the hard, dry earth.

At this early hour the wind was absent and the whole valley, all sharpness smeared away by the half-light, was a pastel of browns and greys, the sky above it a lighter grey, the dying stars still faintly gleaming. Sometimes during these lonely patrols Crown pondered over the wild chance that had brought him to this place, all that lay behind him in his hard, often bitter life, and what might lie ahead. He could no longer feel any more sanguine than anyone else about what might lie ahead after these merciless seasons in the territories, for all hope seemed to have evaporated along with the water, gone away with the creaking wagons and with men and women whose heads were bowed, moving from a nothing, nowhere-landscape towards a barren horizon under the blaze of the sun, flayed all the way by wind-hurled grit.

Crown thought of his own plan to cross the Flinter Hills, two of whose outflung fingers now enclosed him, seeking something better, survivable, up around Saffron. That, too, would be a gamble. And each morning, when he returned from his soft-footed surveillance, it was always to discover that Rebecca was up and washed and cleanly dressed, setting about preparing breakfast.

"Nothing?"

A slight shake of his head.

So the days went sliding by, and minimally, as each one yielded still nothing to Crown's careful, early scouting, the worst of the tension began to drain away. He now became aware that, covertly, she was studying his looks, his movements, the way he spoke and acted in all of their trivial exchanges; and he for his part, and though he believed he took good care to conceal it, observed her too, and was sometimes astonished and disturbed by a glance, an aspect of her appearance, standing near a window or a lamp, caught by some instant's accident of light that made her hair shine the more, her blue eyes sparkle, her creamy skin glow. Crown, in his time, had come across many handsome women but thought that this girl was, when her features were no longer stiff with anxiety, standing for a moment, caught perhaps by some fleeting, far-off fancy, astonishingly beautiful, yet seemingly unaware of it.

On one occasion, after he had watched her handling the rifle, hefting it, sighting it, she surprised him.

"I didn't shoot to hit him. Did you know that? The man you call Eyebrows."

"I thought about it. I thought, after, that if you'd wanted to hit him, even a moving target, as he was, you could have done it. I told him you would with the next one."

"Here I am, carrying this rifle everywhere I go, yet if it came to it, I still don't know if I could shoot *at* a man or not. Does that dishearten you Jim, or make you angry?"

"No," said Crown. "In all my life I never knew anybody anywhere who was even close to a real human being that felt they could do it. But circumstances can change much faster than you'd believe possible. So if it should come to pass, if it's all on an' shouting, if it's a matter of you or him, you'll do it. You must." She nodded and he knew that she accepted what he said. "But if I'm not here, don't let him push you into a hurried shot. Be quite certain that when you shoot, you drop him

136

hard, for you'll stand no chance at all if you don't."

She regarded him soberly and as he turned away he thought that an involuntary shudder had passed through her slim body.

So they continued to pursue their regimen of quiet caution, looking before they went out, and when they were outside, maintaining as great a watchfulness as the ever-present moving dust would permit. That was what worried Crown the most, the dust. A rider, if he were shrewd enough, could use it to advantage, get in reasonably close with a real possibility that, no matter how cautious they were, they would not see him until it was too late. And Crown reasoned also, though he hesitated to say so to Rebecca, that in those circumstances a man with such an element of surprise in his favour would try to take out the one with the lethal rifle first. But as time went on and they were left unvisited he came to think less often in such terms.

In the pale dawn of the fourteenth day, Crown, dressed and with the long gun hung on him, moved a curtain, raised his window and unlatched the shutters, opening them far enough to look out; and there they were. Whether or not Grieve was among them could not be discerned for they were some distance from the house and in the soft pearl light between night and morning; but whoever they were, there were four of them.

9

THOUGH tension had returned suddenly to grip them both, Crown was aware of the softness of her presence. She had flung on a long, dark blue robe over her nightdress. Her rich, wheat-coloured hair hung between her narrow shoulders but she had taken time to gather it together at the nape of her neck with a scrap of black velvet. The faintest puffiness showed beneath her large eyes and there was a mild flush in her cheeks and some small marks in her soft skin where she had been sleeping on strands of hair; and she still exuded a trace of musty warmth from her bed. She had brought with her, moving almost silently on her narrow, bare feet, both spyglass and rifle. The rifle she put on Crown's still-rumpled bed, and when he nodded at the partly-opened shutters she extended the spyglass and moved it along slowly until she reached the group of men and horses. Several times however she lowered the glass and rubbed at her eyes and finally, handing it to Crown, said:

"Here. You look. I've too soon come out of sleep to see properly. And the light outside is still poor."

He nodded, took the instrument from her and moved to take her place at the window. Rebecca, however, still stood close behind him, craning to see whatever she could, and as he propped his elbows on the sill, holding the spyglass steady, he felt the light touch of her hand on his shoulder.

"Is it him? Is it Billy Grieve?"

Crown did not answer immediately for he had set about trying to examine each of the distant men in turn, and he was glad that they were not on the move but were sitting their horses, occasionally looking in the direction of the homestead, but mostly talking among themselves. If they had realized that they were possibly being watched they seemed to be singularly unconcerned about it. The horses were shaking their heads, sometimes tossing them, moving restlessly, and Crown, through the imperfect, shuddering disc of the spyglass had some difficulty in fastening successfully on the faces of the men; but he persevered and at last, one by one, got a reasonably clear look at each of them. When he had accomplished this he scrutinized the rough clumps of brush just off to one side of them.

"I can't see Grieve; but I do recognize two of them." Then: "Wait." She saw him make a slight adjustment to the spyglass and keep quite still. "Ah, I thought so." There was another horse out there just beyond the brush, and now the dismounted rider, buttoning his trousers, walked into view, the horse following docilely, its reins looped over the man's left shoulder. "Grieve's there, all right. So there are five of them."

"The others, the two you say you

recognize, who are they?"

"Their names I never did find out, but I met them not long before I came here, between Hope and Albertine." Again he peered through the glass. "They're on the move."

"Coming here?" She was unable to keep the anxiety out of her voice.

"No, they're just walking the horses to the left, in among the brush, going out of sight." He stared through the glass a moment or two longer, then straightening up, snapped it shut. "I don't know what it is they're up to but at a guess I'd say we'll see more of them before too much longer."

"The two you recognized, where did you meet them?"

"Not in good circumstances." He told her about the Sellers family and their wagon and the death of the black-bearded man. "If Grieve's told 'em that I'm here, and I've no doubt he will have, they'll be real anxious to square that matter." Crown did not add that, because of what had nearly taken place at the Sellers' wagon before he had intervened, Rebecca Parr stood in greater danger than ever; and indeed if he were to be knocked out of this, he did not care to contemplate what would happen to her.

"I'll get dressed." She went padding away out of the room leaving Crown once more to move to the window and resume his watch with the spyglass. They had not reappeared but it now occurred to him that they might well be dispersing so that soon they would have the farm buildings covered from several angles. Then perhaps he would hear from them in no uncertain terms. One thing stood in his favour, though he had to admit that it was only one against many that were not in his favour at all. The homestead and its outbuildings were surrounded on all sides by the flat, bare blocks of land where once the crops had stood and though, beyond these large patches, there was plenty of concealment to be had among brush and large rocks, the

143

range was undoubtedly too great for their pistols to make any impression, if they remained firing from cover.

That meant that, to be effective, they would most certainly have to break cover and come in at him. But the problem was that they could do it simultaneously from five separate points and there was simply no way that even two people, moving from window to window in the main building, could cover every one of them; and eventually at least one of the men might get established in one of the outbuildings.

The sun was beginning to stretch bold fingers across the valley and though Crown believed that it would not be very long before the wind rose and with it the dangerous, enveloping, concealing dust, the light during this period improved markedly and Crown took the opportunity to scrutinize afresh the segment of land that lay before him.

Rebecca came back into the room wearing a green dress with a white collar and with her hair now drawn up and secured at the back. Crown said that it was now time for them to visit each window in turn, raise them to their fullest extent and open and secure the shutters, taking a good look in each direction. They must do this at every window except the one which directly faced the wind; that one would have its shutters opened but the window itself would need to be closed again against the eventual dust.

"If they rush the house from different positions it's going to be difficult," he said, there being no point in avoiding that fact. "If they do seem to be doing that, try to get around to each window as fast as you can and make a count of the men coming. We have to know as soon as we can if they're all in the open. Keep as much out of the way of the window as you can while you're about it. First off, I'll take the rifle an' try to drop one, an' with any luck, two of 'em coming in."

She nodded and then separately they

went to various windows, released shutters, raised all of the windows that were to be raised, all the while looking carefully out across the open ground. As far as they could see, nothing was stirring and there was, as yet, not much wind. Joining Crown again, Rebecca said:

"I'll prepare some food now. It might be some while before there's another chance to do it." She went into the kitchen.

Crown continued moving from window to window and at one time even went out onto the back porch and took a good look towards each of the outbuildings before retreating inside again.

While Crown ate his breakfast Rebecca took up the task of keeping a regular watch; then they reversed the roles. When both were again free to keep a look out it was Rebecca who, after about a half hour of fruitless watching, called:

"I can see one of them."

Crown arrived quickly, carrying the rifle. Right out on the fringe of the brush, not far from where Crown himself had been in the gunfight, a single rider had emerged and appeared to be walking his horse directly towards the house. Rebecca had got the spyglass and was carefully focussing it on the horseman. Presently, she said:

"It's Grieve."

"He's not travelling very fast," said Crown, "and he doesn't yet have the cover that the dust would give him. It could mean he's coming to talk."

Rebecca said she would go around checking windows in case of the others were also on the move. Crown leaned his left shoulder against the window-frame and, holding the rifle ready, waited. Grieve came slowly on. He was making no signals, simply walking the horse, seemingly holding the reins in both hands. Grieve was now well out into open ground and there was still no sign of anybody else. To Rebecca, wherever she was, Crown called:

"Anything?"

"No." Presently she came back in. "How far away is he now?" Crown handed her the rifle as she came closer to look. "Down to fifty yards. Cover me from here. I'll talk to him outside."

"Jim, be careful."

Crown let himself out onto the porch and went down the steps and around to the corner of the pumphouse and by the time he got that far, Grieve was not much more than thirty yards from the house.

"Far enough!" called Crown.

Grieve pulled the horse to a stop and half-raised one gloved hand, his face splitting into one of his purest smiles.

"Well now," said Billy Grieve, "an' here I was opinin' yuh'd mebbe pulled yore pin an' drifted on, by this."

"Life's filled with disappointments," said Crown.

"Wa — al," said Billy Grieve, glancing around him, relaxed and casual, "it still ain't filled with water." He sniffed, looked briefly at Crown.

"The good li'l lady around?"

"She's here," said Crown. "She's occupied."

"Nevertheless," Grieve said, steadying his horse, "I'd admire to talk with her. Talk with the boss, I allers say. It beats jawin' with the hired help by a good long ways."

"Trust me," said Crown. "Miss Parr does."

"Whee — ow! I jes' bet she does that!" said Grieve, slapping his knee. "Why, I reckon yuh'd be the luckiest damn' farmhand south of Albertine, James. Yessir, I shore do!"

"Well," said Crown evenly, "if that's what you've come all the way back to say, you can now leave. You can get your ass off this land, right out of this valley, in fact, an' stay out of it. It's a big disappointment to me that the same message didn't get taken in the first time."

Grieve blew his cheeks out, then smiled, looked at Crown then away.

"Yuh might live to regret all that,

Crown. Then again, yuh might not."
Crown stepped clear of the corner
and Grieve again raised one hand
but slowly. "O.K, O.K, I'm goin'.
But you mind what I say, hired help.
Think about it."

Crown said in a firm, hard voice, his
unyielding gunmetal stare fixed firmly
on Billy Grieve:

"The whole five of you can come on
in any time now. But you think about
this. At least one will be dead before
you're all across the open ground, even
if the dust blows up. Two more will be
shot close in to the house; an' if what's
left still have enough sand to get inside,
then that's where they'll die. Tell those
two shitbags that were at the wagon
between Hope and Albertine that, for
like as not they'll be the first to sight
the portals of Hell."

Grieve had been in the act of turning
his mount away but had frozen, lips
pulled back from his white teeth in what
was only the travesty of a smile and his
face had become chalky. Nevertheless

he threw off the shock quickly and favoured Crown with a look of pure malevolence. When he spoke his voice was husky with malice.

"Crown, my time'll come. Be sure of it."

"Not with me, boy," said Crown, "because I'll never turn my back on you. Now move."

Abruptly Grieve hauled the horse all the way around and departed the way he had come. Crown watched him for maybe half a minute then went back in the house. Rebecca was still near the window holding the rifle but keeping it low down, out of the way.

"I stayed back," she said, "though I could still see him all the time. He looked towards the window once but I don't believe he saw me. He certainly wouldn't have seen the rifle."

Crown nodded, pleased.

"Well, now we wait." He knew that this could almost be the worst time.

"The wind's beginning to come up," she said. It was true. Crown could see that, as he went, the retreating horseman was raising some light dust which was at once being skimmed away in a thin film.

Crown sighed, drew the long pistol, broke the cylinder out, examined it, snapped it shut, slid the big gun away. With the faintest of smiles he said:

"Today was the day I was going to say the danger was past. I was going to suggest that I leave here and cross the Flinters an' go on up to Saffron to try for some supplies, an' pack them back here. I would have been away for a touch over two weeks."

Rebecca glanced at him, then took up the glass once more. Of Grieve she said:

"He's gone." Then: "How long do you think it will be before they try?"

"I doubt it will be before the dust gets thicker."

"What you said to him. Might it make them think again?"

"Yeah, I reckon it might. They'd know they couldn't all get to here alive. But in the end it won't make any odds. They'll still come."

Without looking at him, busying herself with the glass, she said:

"Could they wait it out, wait for us to make some move?"

It was more in the nature of a hope that she was expressing, he knew, than a belief, for she was nothing if not intelligent.

"No, I think not. We've got food here, though they don't know how much — or how little. They do know that we've got plenty of water. That's the key. It's my bet that they've got very little of either, food or water, among the lot of them. So they can't afford to let it run on for long; in fact, from their point of view, the sooner they move the better, and when they do, they'll give it a real hard try."

After a short silence, she said:

"It might be that they have more ammunition than we do."

Crown nodded. "That's the real problem. Somehow, we'll need to balance that." A half-plan had already formed in his mind but it depended a good deal on chance, so he did not broach it. What he did say to her was: "They'll do a lot of shooting on the way in and not all of it will be good because they might begin when the range is against them, and even within range, accurate shooting from a moving horse is almost never possible. But there'll still be a lot of lead coming. When it starts, get down on the floor for safety. If you have to check from a window, do it quick and get down quick."

"Do you think they will split up, come singly?"

"There are arguments for it. As they'll know, it would stretch us to defend against that sort of attack. Against it, though, is the risk of them hitting one of their own, if by then it's not possible to see clearly. They sure won't come bunched up, but they might try a feint; I mean that some of them, strung out wide, might come fast towards the house, probably downwind, increasing the dust that would be blown ahead of them, while others come from another direction, not opposite, but across maybe at right angles. The dust, if it gets worse, can help them, but it can help us too. None of them would want to ride directly into it, not for long, anyway; and I can tell you, riding across it is no good experience either. If you want something to hope for, hope the wind begins to blow harder."

It did. Not so long after Crown had expressed that thought, a gust funneling down the valley buffeted the house, and a rolling curtain of dust and grit went rushing across the open ground. Crown went to the window, the one still completely closed but rattling in the onset of the wind, and pondered the problem that he would have, of seeing any horsemen approaching through the shielding clouds, much less managing to get a shot at any of them in the teeth of it all. He decided that, in the event, provided that he saw them in time, he must raise the window just sufficiently for the rifle to be poked through and so that the glass would still partially shelter him and hope that it would not be shattered by a bullet.

Minutes passed; too, fifteen, twenty, and still they did not come. Rebecca, returning from her rounds of other windows, shook her head at his enquiring glance. She was pale but calm and he had no sense of failing nerve on her part; yet there was about her, young and slim and light of carriage, a frailty that he was also deeply aware of, and the thought of her falling into the hands of the kind of men who were out there and to whom the deeds in prospect would mean little or nothing, appalled him. If he had fear it was certainly for Rebecca. Perhaps she did read something of that in his eyes, for she made some effort towards normality, vanishing for some short while, returning with a mug of steaming coffee. Crown sipped it gratefully. Rebecca went back to her routine of watching. Time drifted on. Crown finished his coffee, squinted into the bowling dust, rifle ready, but still they did not come. More than fifty minutes had elapsed since Grieve had withdrawn and the gusty wind had risen. When Rebecca reappeared, now looking a little more tense, Crown said:

"This will be part of it, making us wait, keeping us guessing. They'll know we can't relax, stop watching for them. It could well go on for hours." But it had begun to trouble Crown to a greater degree than he was prepared to admit to Rebecca; for if they should be made to wait, in growing tension, until the afternoon, perhaps even until late in the day, they would face a night in which their eyes would be burning with weariness, yet through which at least one of them would be compelled to remain awake. All he said to the girl, however, was: "It could turn into a long wait, so we'll need to rest whenever we can, as much as we can. You should do that now." If she had not reached all the same conclusions that Crown had done, she was smart enough to grasp the implications of what he said, for she at once complied:

"Of course." She withdrew and he assumed that she had settled herself elsewhere in the house, conserving her energy against the time when it would be needed.

Crown did not relax his own vigilance. He was convinced he had chosen the right place to wait for the first sight of them, and was now content to allow matters to take their course. There was no more that he could do. He found that constant watching did indeed become wearing and the quarter-hours went dragging by, filled with only the thumping sound of the hot wind against the homestead and the monotonous banging of something loose on one of the outbuildings, and the unchanging sight of oncoming, impenetrable dust.

Inside the house itself though, all had fallen quiet, there being no sound from

Rebecca, and there settled upon Crown a sense of isolation, of having somehow arrived at the end of some important trail and of now having to prepare himself to face one maybe final trial in a long succession of hardships that had been his lot in a country now almost bereft of life and bereft indeed of law and common decency. How quickly, mused Crown, does the edifice of order begin to crack and crumble when men are pressed, through desperation, to fall back entirely upon their own resources against the needs and wishes of their fellows. The raw instinct for personal survival knows no niceties and soon brings out the best and worst in all of them; and all too soon brings forth the greedy, bold, malicious and depraved, those shorn of all compassion and restraint. Devil take the hindmost, Crown thought. Then abruptly, his eye, all in an instant, catching sight of something darker in the wall of moving dust, he was shouting:

"Rebecca! They're coming!"

10

AT one moment there had been nothing but the charging dust, the next, the mounted men; two . . . three of them, fifty yards away and closing fast. A bright flash burst out near one of them and there was the heavy sound of a shot but no other noise of anything striking against the house. Crown had raised his window slightly, at once receiving a fierce slash of grit, sudden wind pushing at his shirt as he was crouching ready, but holding his fire.

"There's three here!" he called. "Do you see any?"

"No! No, none!" Her voice sounded firm, certain.

Crown waited an impossible time until they seemed almost atop of the place and knowing that within seconds they must pass out of his line of vision to go tearing by along the side of the house, the nearest of them perhaps fifteen yards from it, and as he pumped one shot away, the dry timbers of the old homestead were pounded in a thunderous strike of lead as their pistols boomed; and then the riders were gone. Only a scant few seconds had elapsed between the moment of his first seeing them and the moment of their disappearance.

Crown slammed his window shut but resisted the impulse to go running through the house in an effort to catch further sight of them, maybe blast another shot, relying on the good sense of the girl to tell him what their movements were. Instead, Crown waited, his whole attention again on the boiling dust. He had seen three go by. Rebecca had not seen the others. He knew there were five out there somewhere. The girl called:

"They've ridden on by, almost gone now; but there are only two . . . no,

161

wait . . . " Then: "Three horses, only two riders."

So he had hit one of them. If it had not been Grieve himself, then he hoped that Grieve remembered what he had told him. Then suddenly the missing two were there. They were not close together, either, but were riding even harder than had the first ones, and even as Crown saw the dark shapes of them, his window burst asunder and he was covered in tearing grit and shards of flung glass, diving to the floor, turning his face from the scoring blast, aware that he was cut but not knowing how badly. Soon he heard Rebecca calling that she saw two more riders, going away, and when she came to the door of the room, could not suppress a small cry as she felt the thrash of wind and saw that he was down.

He was cut above the left eyebrow and on the back of one of his hands, but not badly, though in spite of that there did seem to be a good deal of sticky blood on his face. He got to his feet, handed her the rifle and then, crossing to the window, head turned half away, feeling blindly, reached around and released first one shutter, then the other. Struggling with them, he then closed and secured them both.

"It was a poor scheme at best," Crown said. "I'll have to find some better way of watching this side." He nodded towards the other part of the house. "Best make sure there's no more sign of 'em."

She slipped away but presently returned, shaking her head. She wet a cloth with cold water from a pitcher and wiped the blood away from Crown's hand and forehead, then fetched some thick salve and smeared it on his cuts.

"There's one of them down some-where," said Crown. He went to an open window at the side of the house, cupping one hand to shield his eyes, trying to pierce the murky clouds being blown on by. "Maybe when he came down he rolled closer to the house; or maybe even got away. In this filth you'd never know. I don't know how hard I hit him. I'll have to go take a look."

"Go out?" This time there was a touch of alarm in her tone, and the clear blue eyes searching his face were filled with apprehension.

"Whether he's alive or dead," said Crown, "he'll likely have some ammunition on him. We need to get our hands on that and do it before any of them come back. And they will be back." Crown put on his hat and thonged it firmly underneath his chin. His bandanna he took off and soaked in water, then tied it back on in such a way that it would cover his nose and mouth. "Just stay alert," Crown said to her. "The one outside can't be far away so I'll not be gone long."

He stepped to the open window and swung one leg over the sill, then the other and as soon as he was out, was sent staggering by a ferocious gust and the wide brim of his hat was flattened against his face. Nevertheless he backed against the side wall of the homestead and began edging along sideways into the teeth of the wind, knowing that he must eventually go backing into it, and knowing also, that doing it would render him open to attack if the man who had been hit was indeed nearby and still able to shoot. But by the time Crown reached the corner of the house, he saw him.

He was perhaps fifteen yards out, lying as though he had fallen asleep, chest down, head turned so that one side of his face was on the ground. The wind was tearing at him, wildly fluttering loose clothing, and he was almost completely shrouded in fine dust. Crabbing across to him, making very slow progress in doing it, he then stooped and with a strong effort, grasping a shoulder with both hands, managed to turn him face up. Crown did not recognize him. He had been hit full in the upper chest, and nearly all of the front of his ragged green shirt was darkened with blood. He had a thickset body and thinning, sandy hair — for there was no hat in evidence — and his clothing was old and had many holes in it. Saddletramp by the looks of him, possibly seeing some opportunity in siding the likes of Billy Grieve, or even perceiving some personal aggrandisement in coat-tailing him. Well, whatever the reason and whoever he was, it had brought him to his death. Crown unbuckled the man's shellbelt and tugged it free from under him. The holster was empty, the pistol having fallen somewhere, probably from the man's hand, but Crown was not concerned about it.

Fewer than five minutes had elapsed when, to Rebecca's profound relief, Crown reappeared at the window, slung the shellbelt and holster in and climbed in after them.

"Unknown," said Crown, "and dead." The dozen or so .45 loads in the shellbelt were, after all that, thin pickings, but better than nothing. "So now they're four," he said, "and maybe after that they'll try something different."

"Different? But they must still cross open ground whatever they do."

"True," Crown said. "But we have a blind spot if they can get to it. They might not realize that yet, but whether or not they do, I doubt they'll come back at us riding into this damn' wind. They'd have to be loco to try it, for we could pick them off one by one as soon as they came into sight, being held back by the wind and blinded by the dust. No, they'll circle, afoot and leading the horses, like as not, work around upwind again and do what they ought to have done the first time."

"What?"

"Come in fast, behind the out-buildings, get set up there and start blowing some holes in this place."

Her face had gone very pale and she half raised her long, slim hands, then let them fall to her sides.

One other matter now troubled Crown as he went through to the closed shutters at the broken window. Though it was several hours away he was concerned about what might have to be faced after sundown. Though the wind would fall away, the night would become clear and probably brightly illumined by the moon. If by that time they had got themselves into the outbuildings it would become very dangerous indeed for those inside the homestead, with perhaps few opportunities to shoot back without becoming too exposed. However, he did not have time to think about it any more, for more urgent matters intruded. They had circled, right enough. Through a narrow gap in the shutters, one hand raised to protect his eyes, he only just caught the flicker of movement across the open ground beyond the outbuildings. Crown, making up his mind that he might as well take a crack at them, unlatched one shutter, thrust one elbow to it against the pressing of the wind, and shot at one of them.

It was impossible for him to tell whether or not he had got his man, for another wave of dust swept at the window and Crown had to let go the shutter and duck his head away, eyes feeling the fiery sting of grit. Rebecca was at hand almost at once with a dampened cloth and Crown wiped at his eyes, blinking, clearing them. He handed the cloth back to her.

"There was no way I could prevent them getting in the shelter of the buildings. All I do know is that all four seem to be there, so for now, there's no threat from another direction. But now we'll need to keep plenty of wood between us and them." Hardly had he finished saying it than several slugs came slamming at the outer walls, and one smashed a ragged hole in the loose window shutter and buried itself in the opposite wall. Crown hurried Rebecca from the room even as another shot blew more pieces from the shutter, which would now be past any usefulness, so that the force of the windstorm rendered Crown's earlier position there untenable.

Rebecca took charge of the rifle. Crown moved through to where there was an open side window and from it he could see the barn and part of the yard and the nearest outbuilding to the barn. Slowly, watching carefully, Crown leaned out, dust swirling past him, but he was unable to see any of the men doing the shooting and neither did he draw any fire. Now he believed he knew where they all must be. There was a long shack which housed a plough and other farm implements and next to it, a lean-to, then the smaller shack in which in earlier days Crown had discovered the adze and spade which he had used to dig Evelyn Parr's grave.

He could not see the horses belonging to Grieve and the others so assumed that all four must be hitched where their riders had dismounted before breaking into the shacks, and where the mounts would be at the present time, still unprotected from the full blast of the dust storm. Crown believed that men who, as part of their daily existence, depended heavily on the horses and as a part of a routine took good care of them, would not permit them to remain so exposed for very long. They would try to get them into the barn; and if they did that, they would find, as well as the two horses already in there, the sufficiency of feed. And the water in the trough.

Crown thought about it, putting himself in their boots. What would he do? He reckoned that he would not expose everyone but, again, would certainly not mount just one man up to tow all the animals to the barn, so that man would have to dismount to open the tall doors and lead them all inside. No, he would more likely have a man run from nearest cover, unlatch the doors and open them and get inside as fast as he possibly could. Then the second man would run the horses in. Once that was accomplished, the seige could settle down in earnest. Quietly, he said to Rebecca.

"I'll need the rifle, I reckon." She handed it to him and he told her what his theory was.

More than a half-hour he waited, kneeling near the open window, rifle held ready. Spasmodic shooting was coming from the concealed men, slugs hanging into the back porch and totally demolishing the window shutters. But when there occurred a longer-than-usual pause in the shooting, Crown at once read it as a result of their becoming occupied with other matters and he thought he heard, carried on the wind, the sound of horses whickering. When that came to him he fastened his attention on the gap between the farthest outbuilding and the barn, and the barn itself. Dust was funnelling through that gap, whipping, rolling, sometimes almost totally obscuring the entire front of the big barn.

He acknowledged to himself that it would be a difficult matter to see anything, at times, and that there was a strong element of chance stacked against him.

But it was the red shirt that the man was wearing that gave him away and though Crown did not see him clearly until he had actually arrived outside the barn doors, a figure bending his shoulders and face down as the wind and grit tore at his clothing, he did see him with reasonable clarity then, struggling with the wooden locking bar. Crown, though concerned not to allow the doors to be opened, took his time sighting the rifle, much aware of the effect that the strong wind would have on a bullet travelling across it, then squeezed the shot away.

Just as he fired, a thicker dust-cloud obscured not only his target but most of the barn as well; but when it thinned, Crown, to his satisfaction, could see that the tall doors had not been opened and that the red-shirted man was a huddled shape up against them. After shooting, Crown had withdrawn slightly, motioning to Rebecca to retreat from the room, and it was just as well that he adopted such prudence; for one or more of them must have got themselves along nearer to the barn, probably because of the horses, and had quite quickly deduced where the killing shot had come from. A storm of pistol fire hammered into the side of the house, and inevitably, two or three of the slugs came whipping into the room where Crown was, pounding into the wall behind him. He called to Rebecca, now out of his sight:

"Are you all right?"

"Yes." He was immensely relieved to hear her voice.

"Now there are three of them. I doubt they'll try again for the barn, unless they do it after sundown."

They did not make another attempt but must have worked out what Crown's options were in so far as his range of fire was concerned, and so spread themselves that they then produced, from different positions, a slow but steady fire, some of it directed at the back porch and at the already-ravaged shutters, some at the side window from which Crown had shot the man in the red shirt. Crown himself did not often respond, and when he did it was with little hope of hitting any of them, more a continuing declaration of his wakefulness and watchfulness. Yet as the day came towards its close and Rebecca prepared some food, he regarded the prospect of a long night with some anxiety. When finally the sun did sink away and the dangerous shadows of early evening invaded the yard and all the buildings around it, he became especially watchful. They could light no lamps; that would have been suicidal.

The wind had fallen right away, and Crown regarded the rising of the huge moon with mixed feelings. Deep shadows served some purpose in that, when those outside fired at the house he was able to see by the stab of flame where each one was crouching; and the front of the barn where the red-shirted man still lay was bathed in milky light. In such luminosity they would not move out into the yard; yet no more could Crown.

"We've come full circle," he murmured to Rebecca, smelling the warm scent of her near him in the darkness, for it had been on just such a night as this that Crown had come here, confronting other enemies. He felt the gentle pressure of her hand on his arm, a gesture needing no words.

It was about this time that they became aware of omniscient silence, almost an eerie stillness, and after a little time Crown conducted a slow and stealthy tour of the house, watching, listening, trying to decide if the men outside were on the move, perhaps endeavouring to circle around and close in. Presently he came back to where he had started, saw the pale heart shape of her face in the gloom. It was at that moment that they heard the horses. Crown, going to the window, saw nothing, then realized that the sounds were diminishing and that to see anything at all he would have to go into the back room, to the shutters where he had first stood when they had come riding out of the dust.

"Wait here, Rebecca. Watch the yard and the barn."

He strode through to the back room and once there looked through what remained of the shutters. He could still hear the horses but at first could see nothing. Then out across the open ground, but almost merging into the dark background of the more distant brush, there they were, horsemen, but no longer discernible individually, merely a dark bunch, going further away. After a little time the riders vanished and all fell quiet, Crown went back to where Rebecca waited.

"They've gone? I mean, they've pulled back?" she asked.

Crown drew a deep breath. "Maybe

they have, maybe not. They'd have us think so, anyway." Both of their faces caught in the wash of the moon, he looked at her. "They could have left one man behind."

"To watch?"

"To kill me if I should go outside." And he hardly needed to add: "But go I must, to make sure; then see to our horses." The rifle was to remain with Rebecca. Crown would leave the house by a window on the opposite side from the yard. "If you should hear gunfire — anything — stay in here. If it's me comes to the house, after, you'll know it. Otherwise, kill whoever it is."

11

HE was in one of the narrow channels that once had been used to carry water to the fields, and to get to it he had had to pass the body of the man shot out of the saddle earlier, and who had now become whitened by blown dust.

Clogged as the channel had become with dried grass and spiky weeds and thick as it was with silt blown in over so many scorching months, Crown, by lying full-length and edging himself along on knees and elbows, was able to make some progress without showing himself. But it was exceptionally hard going and it was not long before his knees and his arms became bruised, scored and sore, until in fact there was a real temptation to gain some relief by standing up. Yet to have done so would have invited instant attention from anyone who had been left behind for precisely such an eventuality. So Crown gritted his teeth and inched his way along, knowing that he must make quite sure that by the time he paused and risked a look he must have worked himself into a position beyond the outbuildings.

There was an absolute stillness on this magnificent night and Crown became conscious of even the slightest sound that he made in working his way along the channel; for such sounds, unavoidable and slight though they were, seemed, in these conditions, to be magnified. And he could not prevent his thoughts returning from time to time to Rebecca Parr, left alone in the homestead. Whatever the events of this night dictated he must do, he knew he must do his utmost to prevent any attack upon her. Yet if the horsemen came back while he was still outside, then he might be left with few options. It might have to come down to a shoot, and that was a prospect for which he had little enthusiasm for he was realist enough to know that a fight with such an imbalance of numbers to it, out in the open, could have but one outcome, no matter if some of the luck ran with him.

Now he rested for perhaps a minute, his legs and arms aching and his elbows, in particular, afire from constant scraping as he had been inching his way along; but he knew that he must persist. He was not yet far enough along to risk easing up out of the shallow trench and he could not gamble and make a mistake. The moon shone with white brilliance and anyone in the full flood of it would stand out across some fair distance. That presented Crown with a threat which he could not avoid, for whenever he chose to emerge he would have to cross an area that was brightly lit.

He worked his way along for another five yards and decided that this was it; it was now or never. With great care he raised his head and upper body and looked first to his right. He was gratified to discover that his judgement had not been far astray. The backs of the outbuildings were clearly to be seen some sixty feet from where he was, a long block of obsidian shadow. With infinite caution Crown now turned his head and stared across the open ground towards the ragged blackness of the distant brush and the large rocks that lifted into the farther side of the valley. Over there, nothing; but he was convinced that there were hidden eyes across there. Nevertheless he must now do what he had set out to do.

Slowly he eased up and out of the trench, began to crawl, in bright moonlight, towards the backs of the farm buildings. Crown had to dismiss from his mind any fears that he might by now have been seen by those in the brush, far off though they might be; and of course, if one man had been left behind here, he might simply be waiting for Crown to approach to within a range at which it would be impossible to miss him. That thought too, had to be firmly suppressed. He was out, he was moving in white light and during these moments felt that he was in as much raw danger as he had ever been in his lifetime of danger. Still there came no sound, no sudden cry, no booming gunshot, no stab of flame out of the darkness.

On he crawled, conscious of the fact that from time to time a boot struck a stone or scuffed on hard earth. No matter, nothing could repair those errors; he must simply press on. He was totally committed. An age seemed to go by, though in reality it was only a very few minutes before he came within reach of the sharp black shadows behind the nearest of the shacks. Still nothing stirred and with immense relief Crown crawled out of the sharp and lethal moonlight and lay for a few moments recovering himself, realizing only now that his hands were filmed with sweat. He sat against the dry, hard wall of the shack, drying his palms on his shirt. So far, so good. He glanced across the open ground, shining and empty. Stiffly, Crown stood up. Steel whispered softly on old leather as he drew the long pistol.

Risking the sharp metallic sound, he cocked it. Then he began to go along quietly behind the shacks, moving through shadow, pausing from time to time to listen, allowing the men who had come here to clamber inside. Crown checked each one out but discovered no-one. Finally, there was but one remaining, the one nearest the barn. Crown heard nothing, but for a moment as he stood surveying it he had a strong feeling that this was it. This was the trap. Crown drew in a long breath, held it for the count of four, softly expelled it, repeated the ritual twice. His whole body, every nerve, was now quite still. When he heard the horse blowing he realized that he had miscalculated, that his man was here right enough, but not inside this shack. He was further on, in the shadow of the barn, or even at the farther end of it, and even as Crown looked, the gun-flash came and lead whispered by; and as Crown himself shot, tall and hard in the gun-flicker, a horse and rider went plunging away out from the blanket of the shadows at the barn's far corner into sharp moonlight, the man shooting again, bringing a loud sound of impact on the planks a good two yards away from Crown.

Crown took his time, levelling the pistol, swinging ahead of the target, the rider on the now-running horse that was cutting across at an angle, galloping over the barren ground, rapidly opening the range; and even as Crown's pistol bucked and flashed he knew he had not got a clean hit; but he had nicked him, for he heard the cry and the rider seemed to sway sightly as he rode. But he bent again to his task, spurring the horse onward and Crown did not waste another shot. Yet in the few crowded, frantic moments, from the instant the man had bounded the horse out of shadows, to the full-blooded running across the open land, Crown had gained the impression, from the general cast of him, that he had seen him before. It came to him then. The Sellers wagon. The weedy freckled man who had been holding the horses.

Crown swore under his breath. He had had a real chance to reduce the odds and had failed to do it, for even though he was reasonably sure that he had hit the rider, Crown did not believe that he had hurt him badly. There was no point, however, in pondering the issue. Crown slid the pistol back in its holster and lost no time in approaching the doors of the barn. There, he bent over the dusty body of the red-shirted man and from it gathered the eight bullets that were in the shellbelt, and from the man's Colt pistol gained a further four. Crown put all of these into his pockets then stopped and, taking the man by the ankles, hauled him out clear of the doors.

Turning as he heard a noise, Crown

saw the pale shape of Rebecca Parr who had come out onto the back porch of the house and he caught the gleam of the rifle barrel. Crown raised one hand, knowing that he would be clearly recognizable in the light of the moon. He then unbarred the doors and opened them wide to allow the spill of the moon into the barn and went inside. The trough still had sufficient water in it. He topped up the feed troughs, rubbed the smooth necks of both animals, then heard the girl call and went out quickly, swung the doors to, dropped the bar back into place.

"Jim! They're coming back!"

He heard them now. Rebecca was in the yard. He jogged across and joined her. It was true; they were coming. He could not only hear them now, he could see them, all three. Crown took the rifle from her, gently steered her towards the house, then turning, went to the corner of the building to stand in black shadows there, waiting. They were still bunched up. He brought the rifle to his shoulder and blasted a shot away and the immediate effect was to see them spread out, plainly visible in the bright night, one coming on, the one on either flank veering away sharply. Crown shot again and this time the oncoming horseman, evidently alarmed, swung away, gun flaming as he did so, and the others went curving away too, in opposite directions until, eventually, going further away, they rejoined and together withdrew to a point some two hundred yards distant and there, drew to a halt, looking towards the farm.

With his rifle, Crown had given them something to chew on but he was disappointed that he had failed to draw blood; and though he had clipped one of them earlier, it had clearly not impaired the man's ability to ride. For want of sleep Crown's eyes were burning now, but he knew that as long as he kept a watch, the riders would not be able to come back, anyway for as long as the moon was up, and reoccupy any of the farm buildings. At sun-up, and when the wind again began to blow, it would be another story. He called to Rebecca and she came out.

"They're out across there," said Crown, pointing. "As long as I keep watch they can't come in again. Even at that range I could let go with the rifle but this is no light for shooting; and anyway, I prefer to have them stay where I can see them. So one of us has to stay awake through the night. Best you get some sleep now an' you can let me sleep later."

"Give me two hours, no more," she said, "then I'll watch them."

He nodded and she went back into the house.

After ten minutes or so the group of riders began to walk their horses across at an angle, not approaching, but obviously examining the farm, like predators circling a grazing herd, seeking a way to come closer for the kill, yet still wary of doing so. Crown even hoped that they might, at least once, yield to the temptation, and vowed to himself to empty at least one of the saddles if they did make the attempt. But they had stopped again.

For the next hour Crown was compelled to move from place to place to ensure that he kept them in view, for they continued the strange business of shifting about, then pausing for a time before again moving on. Now he was feeling quite acutely the lack of sleep, yet believed that the horsemen out there must surely be in little better shape; and it was, it seemed to him, almost as though this thought of his must have, in some odd way, communicated itself to the night riders, for at that moment he saw that they were moving away. Not hurriedly, to be sure, but they were going. Unswervingly Crown kept his eyes on them until he could no longer be certain whether he could still detect movement or not, then with great relief, sat down with his back against the house and laid the rifle on the ground beside him. He must remain awake, but at least the distance between the enemy and the Parr farm had increased considerably.

He opened his eyes and Rebecca was there, slim, exuding a faint perfume, long cool fingers touching his cheek. Crown got up, shaking his head, knowing how vulnerable he had been. She took up the rifle and all but propelled him towards the house.

Crown fell into a limp sleep. When he came again to consciousness the sun was well risen, the dust was rolling across the land again and Rebecca was shaking his shoulder urgently.

"They're back!"

12

HARDLY had Crown swung his feet off the bed on which he had been lying, fully clothed, than the men outside served savage notice of their return in a withering blast of gunfire.

"Down!" he shouted to Rebecca and half-flung her to the floor as splinters of wood flew and in the nearby kitchen some crockery burst into pieces. Crown himself, not pausing to pick up the rifle, went rolling through the doorway into the kitchen, pistol in one hand, slamming against the far wall, then coming to his knees at the window, was booming two shots away at an already vanishing shadow in the moving dust, gunsmoke swirling in the room, the acrid stench of burnt powder in his nostrils.

Before he cottoned on fully to the

fact that they had not all gone by yet, another misty shadow loomed outside, much nearer than any had come yesterday, and more lethal lead slugs came smashing into the room, breaking more crockery, and Crown shot again and then again. But it was like shooting at wraiths, something less than human, come out of the terrible desert. On the opposite side of the house more bullets were striking and he heard the rifle go off with a deafening report in the confines of the house. He ran to her. She was kneeling, the rifle in her hands, her face ashen, some strands of her hair plastered to a sheen of perspiration on her cheek. Smoke hung in this room too. Crown placed a hand on one of her small shoulders and she managed the faintest of faint smiles.

"One of them went by close to the window."

And then the riders were gone. There was nothing now except the moaning sound of the wind. Crown hurried to the window from which he could look across to the barn. The doors were still closed, the locking-bar still in place. Then he went to collect the rifle and walked through to the back porch. Standing there he took careful aim at one after the other of the outbuildings and pumped a shot into each. There came no answering fire, no response of any kind. Rebecca came to stand behind him. He handed the rifle back to her.

"You'll need to reload it from the box among my things."

"Where are you going?"

"Over there," Crown said, nodding towards the sheds. "I don't think they're there, any of them, but I want to make damn' certain of it."

"Where would they have gone, if not there?"

"Back into the brush, maybe." He looked at her. "Rebecca, I shot away more ammunition than I'd intended to, but I had to let them know that getting in close to the house is a dangerous thing to do, and if they'd

194

come around into those buildings, just as dangerous. For all that it would have been a miracle if I'd hit any of them. Very soon now I'm going to have to work out some way to tip the scales our way. If I can't do that it will only be a matter of time before they make one hard try at us, maybe afoot, and from three sides. If luck ran against us we could have us a real problem. I'm not saying this to alarm you, I'm just giving my opinion of what could happen and what we need to be ready for."

"I understand, Jim. Just tell me what I ought to do and I'll do it."

"Right now," he said, "keep as sharp a look out as you can, in this damn' dust. I'll not be long away."

He went out and across the yard, buffeted by the wind and stung by the grit, bending into it until he got into the lee of the outbuildings. He then carried out a search of them from one end of them to the other and when he had finished it, went back across the yard to the house, and pushed by the wind, arriving at the porch again, said to her:

"All clear."

Rebecca, going in, closing the door behind them, said:

"Another day of waiting, wondering when they'll come again."

"Only if we let it be so," said Crown. He led her to a chair and had her sit down. "Rebecca, we have to take some kind of chance now. We can't pass another day and another night dangling on a string that's being held by them. It's true that they'll need the water quite badly now and they'll have to count on getting it very soon; tonight at the latest. I think it's time we called some of the shots."

"How can we?"

Crown rubbed at the rough stubble on his jaw. His limbs ached and his legs and elbows were afire still from his activities in the narrow trench the previous night and his head swam from lack of sleep. It was for these reasons as well as for any other that he knew he had to make a move because, to delay further, to wait for them, perhaps for several hours, listening, watching, would surely sap his energy to a point where he would not be up to it when they did come. In that event he might not be able to set himself between them and Rebecca Parr. What was now in his mind however was open to error, to chance, and would for a time leave her exposed and, if it went wrong, abandoned, yet he could see no other course that he might take. For to wait, to do nothing, Crown thought, could have but one end.

"I believe they've gone back into the brush. They don't have much stomach for this rifle. I reckon they've set up some sort of camp there, somewhere, in whatever shelter they've managed to find. They'll now rest up, chew the fat — Billy Grieve's good at that — and work out what to do next; then hit us again, when they're ready. I'm going out an' I'm going to try to work my way into the brush, for I've worked out the general direction they come from, and it's dependent on this wind that's blowing; so I reckon I've figured out about where their camp will be." And then he told her what it was he intended to do. When he had finished she stood up and laid a hand lightly on his arm.

"Jim, they're cunning and they're dangerous. I still go cold, thinking of Billy Grieve. It could be suicidal to try it."

"Sitting here waiting could bring us to the same thing," he said. "The part of it that I don't like is having to leave you here for a time, alone. But I don't dare take you with me. There's one thing we can do to try to make it safer for you; close both the doors that lead into this room and push furniture against them on this side. Have food and water, plenty of it, in here, and all the remaining ammunition. You'll be sealed off from the rest of the house and anybody trying to get in here by the window or by shoving through the doors would be asking to be shot. Could you do it if you had to?"

"Yes. Yes, I could do it. I've thought a lot about that in the last few hours. Grieve and the others with him have no sense of decency or morals or compassion. They and other men like them are part of the plague that's come out of this drought, come up out of the death of other things. They're what some men become when law and order breaks down. Oh yes Jim, I could do it."

★ ★ ★

He could not wait for the cloaking anonymity of night, relying on his ability to slip from shadow to shadow; and in any case, to have waited so long would have been, he thought, fatal. And anyway, this time the wind and the dust it carried with it were to be his allies as, up until now they had been the allies of those who had set themselves to destroy him. So he went in full daylight, out into the hot windstorm, and he went afoot. He had quit the homestead by a window and in the room behind him, Rebecca Parr, armed with the rifle, was barricaded; and the room she was in was one which, if all went to plan, would give her, even through the moving dust, a signal of what was taking place away beyond the flat, open farmland.

Crown was again making slow and painful progress along one of the dried-up water channels, but this time would need to press on far beyond the place from which he had emerged the previous night. This time he had a great deal further to go. So far in fact, that before the distance was even halfway covered, it seemed to him that he had been crawling for days and the dust had found its way into every crevice of his skin and inside all of his clothing and he was soaked with sweat, and hurting.

Yet he had to suppress all feelings of pain and discomfort, try to ignore the draining heat, fix his mind upon the single objective, reaching the farther end of this channel he was in, then hoping that he could cover the remaining open ground without being seen. For if they should see him he was a dead man. He had no means of measuring time but by his estimate almost an hour must have passed before he came to the place at which he must either follow the channel at right angles or come up onto the surface of the hard, dry, denuded ground and from there get himself into the jumble of razor-sharp brush and upthrust rocks which he knew lay ahead.

Crown waited a moment or two, head down; then he made his move and he knew that once committed, once he was out in the open, no matter what happened he must not stop, he must keep going and he would either reach the shelter of the brush or he would walk into a bullet. With an effort he came up out of the channel, bracing himself against the assault of the wind and turning his head to one side to protect his eyes, began to go determinedly forward, not pausing, no longer thinking about it, simply advancing pace by pace, pushing against the wind.

Thrashed by flying grit, choking with it, his clothes now almost white with it, Crown blundered on and on with a wooden, implacable determination, like something that was not human. Just when it seemed that in some bizarre way he had miscalculated and was somehow going in a wrong direction, the first arms of brush clawed at him, raked his clothing, tore his shirt, whipped at his face, drawing blood. It was as though the savage land itself had now allied itself with his enemies and was reaching out to check him, hold him fast against their arrival. Crown sank down and half in desperation, half unreasoning anger, forced his way onwards until suddenly a large rock loomed and he crawled in behind it. He was across the open land. Now he tried to recover his faculty for logical thought; to work out where, by his earlier calculations at the homestead, he ought now to be and where, by those same calculations, he believed Billy Grieve and his two surviving companions to be.

There was no time to rethink any part of it now; every minute might count. If they were to be, even at this moment, preparing for another assault on the Parr farm, then he was already too late, and that would mean that Rebecca might be finished, Crown stranded and unable to reach her. So Crown, working on belief and instinct, struck out to his left, trying to avoid the sharp brush as it loomed out of the dust, and travelling now across the thrust of the wind. In this fashion, often battered sideways, he walked for perhaps five minutes, then paused again and sank to his haunches. Now he turned so that the wind was at his back and again began to go forward, often on all-fours, trying to fix in his mind any recognizable features which might be vital on his way back.

The brush seemed denser here, but far from dismaying him, suited his purpose; and it was after he had made his way along for a full five minutes that he stopped suddenly and sank right down, listening. For although the wind was carrying sounds away from him he was sure that he had heard the whickering of a horse. Before him, no more than two yards away, a lump of slab-rock blocked his way, yet just to one side of it was what looked as though it might be a narrow but brush-choked passage. Taking infinite care not to strike either stones or dry brush with a boot and perhaps have a sound carry ahead of him, Crown eased forward until he came to the clogged fissure and tried to see what might lie beyond it.

After a minute or two, when he had all but reached the conclusion that he would never be able to see anything whatsoever on the other side, a vagary of wind, an eddy among the rocks revealed, but only for an instant, a small, clear space. He caught sight of the rump of a picketed horse and the shape of a man in a tall hat, before the dust blew across again. But it had been enough for Crown. He had been right; they were here. Crown began to shuffle back the way he had come, against the wind again now, but keeping as low as he could, to minimize its effect, until he was able to go down into a small depression hard up against a thick brush-clump. Crown, with his back to the wind, crouched very low, making of his own body a small shelter. Now he would give them something to think about.

The first two matches failed, but the third, before it died, smoking, caught some of the fine, dry brush he had gathered in. For a moment nothing more seemed to happen and Crown was on his feet and fighting his way upwind and then cross-wind to his right before the tinder-brush behind him exploded in flame, and when he looked back, the orange, black-tipped fire-storm was sweeping away towards where his enemies were, travelling with breathtaking, enormous speed, gathering its roaring voice as it went. Crown felt compassion for the horses, but that was all. He fought onwards, falling, getting up, slashed by brush, bruised from contact with large stones, choking in the dust, hammered by the unremitting wind until at last he burst out of the brush-line onto the dry, featureless ground.

Even through the gliding curtain of dust, the boiling, urgently-lifting smoke could easily be distinguished and so could the swift orange fury at its source. Even from where he was he could hear the high-pitched, terrified sounds of the horses and it made his skin crawl. And then there they were, indistinct, filmed by dust but now astonishingly, out of the path of the fire, one riderless horse, two . . . no, three; and other blurred shapes, those of mounted men, horses and riders fanning out desperately into open ground, ghostly figures of men whose only thought would be survival.

Still moving, Crown had drawn his pistol, trying but failing to account for all three of them. Then, even Crown, hard man that he was, no stranger to violence, could not avoid a gasp of horror when he saw the man running; for not thirty feet from where Crown was, came a man whose name Crown did not know, but whom he remembered also from the Sellers' wagon. Ollerman, it was; Ollerman, running hard through the dust, heavily afire, screaming as he burned, coming right at Crown, eyes starting from his head, mouth open; and seeing Crown loom out of the murk even as Crown saw him, dying as he ran, and yet in his awful agony, his extremity, pulling the pistol he wore, blasting hopelessly at the eerie shape of Crown, as though in that instant he might have believed him to be the devil come looking for him, Crown shot him, spun him, fiercely burning.

Yet, shrieking, the poor wretch that had been Ollerman came on, pistol now swinging wide, away from his body, until Crown stood and shot him again and punched the blazing mass, the flesh now sagging from hands and face, to the wind-torn earth to blaze up once more, then lie, pouring smoke into the urgent wind, Ollerman gone now from his earthly hell to whatever other hell might be waiting for him.

Crown ran past the smoking body, the wind charged with the deep-sweet smell of it, pistol still in his hand, desperate for a further sight of the riders, for Billy Grieve at least, hearing shots somewhere behind him, would know that the fire had been no accident of nature, and that Crown was out; and if Crown was out, then Rebecca Parr was at the farm alone. Running with the wind, enveloped by the dust, Crown could no longer hear horses nor could he see the shadowy riders, and now he no longer cared whether or not they might have drawn to a halt, waiting for him. He had but one thought in his mind and that was to get back to the house where Rebecca waited.

He ran on. A rifle fired, once. Then he heard the horses and, as he glimpsed them, saw the shapes of the farm buildings too. The riders passed into the yard and were now out of his sight, and because the room where Rebecca was and from which she must have seen them and fired, was on the opposite side of the house, the horsemen had quickly got themselves out of the line of fire.

By the time Crown reached the outbuildings and came around the end one and into the lee of it, the horses were being hauled into the wagon lean-to some sixty feet away. And at that moment the man who was with Billy Grieve saw him and called something to Grieve, who was out of sight, presumably hitching the horses.

Crown fired but missed, then retreated back around the end shack into the force of the wind. He began to work his way along the backs of the buildings. But Grieve and his sidekick anticipated that and one of them — Crown did not know which — showed briefly, a long way off now, near the gap that led through to the barn, and shot at him, but the slug was high, hitting the overhang of the roof above his head. Crown went on however, and pushed his way in through a hole torn in the wall by these men when they had sought to use the shacks to lay siege, and was just in time to see Billy Grieve pass across his line of sight, out in the yard, heading for the house. Giving no more thought to the other man somewhere up near the barn, for it must have been he who fired at Crown and thus gave Grieve his opportunity to make a dash for the house, Crown went out through the front of the shack after Grieve who was just then entering the house from the back porch.

Crown sprinted for the porch even as a Colt banged somewhere behind him and lead whipped alarmingly close as he ran. To himself, Crown gave a grudging nod of respect to Grieve for there was no way that the man could have known that Rebecca was barricaded in a room on the opposite side of the homestead and so could not have seen him coming; for all he had known he could have been going in on top of the rifle.

Crown's boots hit the porch as another slug hammered against the house but he did not even turn to look as he went headlong into the kitchen. Grieve's gunflash came from the hallway but only succeeded in shattering crockery and Grieve had ducked away as Crown fired. Then at a sound he turned and blasted at the man from the yard who had sought to come in from the porch, but Crown missed him and heard him running, perhaps to circle the house to try again. From somewhere else, inside, Billy Grieve was calling:

"Come on now, Rebecca, ol' Billy's

twice the man Crown is! Come git yuh a li'l taste o' Billy!"

Crown entered the passage, crouching low, and was just in time to fire at Grieve slipping through a doorway, even flicking his shirt with the slug, filling the passage with gunsmoke. From the closed room where he had left Rebecca there was no sound. Crown broke out the cylinder of his pistol and began the process of reloading it. He had not finished doing so when he heard Rebecca's voice call:

"Jim!" Incomprehensibly, it had come from somewhere outside near the back of the house and as he turned he realized that Grieve, having gone out by a window must have circled very fast and was now coming into the bullet-riddled kitchen behind Crown, pistol in hand, a wide smile on his face, delighted at catching Crown defenceless, beginning to throw down on him.

Then Billy Grieve, as though kicked by a horse, was slammed sideways under the thunder of a rifle shot and hurled among broken crockery, his pistol sliding away and Grieve putting his hands out against the wall as though trying in some way to grasp hold of it for support, but only sliding down to lean against it, blood all over his shirt. He was breathing short and hard as he turned his face bemusedly towards Rebecca and made an effort to say something, failed, and died.

But Rebecca had not tarried in the doorway and was again out on the porch, rifle at her shoulder. Crown finished his reloading, glanced at Billy Grieve, dead, and walked through to join her. The other man, perhaps having been drawn back towards the house and then changed his mind, was part-way across the yard, obviously heading to where the horses were. Rebecca's call had stopped him in his tracks.

"It's your choice. Stand there and drop that, and live, or take another step and go to join Billy Grieve."

His pistol fell to the ground. Dust

swirled around him.

"Who are you?" Crown called.

"Purdie."

"You're a lucky man, Purdie," Crown said. To the unspoken question, Rebecca said:

"I couldn't stay cowering in that room. The sounds told me there was need of another gun. I climbed out of the window just in time to see Grieve going around the house."

Crown went down the porch steps towards Purdie, a man with dried blood on one sleeve, where Crown had caught him the night before.

★ ★ ★

As he had done with Ollerman at the wagon, Crown made Purdie pack his dead away, leading the laden horses, two bodies slung and tied across one of them, for they kept the horse that had been Billy Grieve's.

"Billy owes us that much," said Crown. Purdie had not wished to take the shockingly burned body of Ollerman but Crown had insisted. "He came here with Billy, he leaves with Billy, an' I don't much care where you bury any of 'em, or even if you don't, as long as you take them out of this valley." Crown had filled Purdie's canteen and the canteens on the other horses. "You're in luck for water, Purdie," he said, "for these hombres won't drink much of theirs." And he saw, to it that the horses themselves were well watered before they left.

After he had gone and all his sombre train, swallowed by the searing dust, down the long valley. Rebecca, her fair hair come loose and splayed about her small shoulders and with strands stuck against her cheek, her eyes heavy from strain and lack of sleep and reddened from blown grit, looked at Crown.

"I told you I could do it if I had to."

"That you did," said Crown. "That you did."

She leaned against him, spent.

215

"When we've slept and we've eaten, I'll take Billy's horse, and the mare, and go across the Flinters, up to Saffron with you, if you've still a mind to, and pack supplies back here, enough to last a while, and try to wait it out."

"You want me to come back here?"

"If you've a mind to."

He had no need to answer her, holding her to him, thinking that perhaps, out of these seasons of death there had come at last a gleam of hope.

THE END